Spitfire

Kate Messner

Kate Messner

North Country Books • Utica, New York

Spitfire

Copyright © 2007
by Kate Messner

ISBN-10 1-59531-018-5
ISBN-13 978-1-59531-018-7

Cover Painting by Gail Smith Schirmer
Illustrations by Martha Gulley
Design by Zach Steffen & Rob Igoe, Jr.

Library of Congress Cataloging-In-Publication Data

Messner, Kate.
  Spitfire / by Kate Messner.
      p. cm.
  Summary: In October of 1776, two twelve-year-olds meet on a ship on Lake
Champlain--Abigail, disguised as a boy while seeking her only living relative,
and Pascal, brought aboard by his stepfather, the captain--and forge a fast
friendship while serving together as soldiers.
  ISBN 978-1-59531-018-7 (alk. paper)
  [1. Friendship--Fiction. 2. Sex role--Fiction. 3. Seafaring life--Fiction. 4.
Orphans--Fiction. 5. Stepfathers--Fiction. 6. Valcour Island, Battle of, N.Y.,
1776--Fiction. 7. Champlain, Lake--History--Revolution, 1775-1783--Fiction.
8. United States--History--Revolution, 1775-1783--Fiction. 9. Diaries.] I.
Title.
PZ7.M5615Spi 2007
[Fic]--dc22
                          2007031244

North Country Books, Inc.
311 Turner Street
Utica, New York 13501
www.northcountrybooks.com

Acknowledgments

I have great appreciation for the many people who helped make *Spitfire* a reality. Thanks to the Lake Champlain Maritime Museum, particularly Erick Tichonuk, who reviewed my manuscript for historical accuracy, and to the people of Holland Patent, New York who helped introduce me to Pascal, especially Wanda Goodrow, Caroline "Connie" Roberts, and Virginia and Edward Wardner.

Thanks to my friends and colleagues who helped with *Spitfire*. Social Studies teacher Mal Cutaiar showed me that history is really about stories. Marjorie Light, a fellow English teacher and friend, helped edit, and Stephanie Gorin, who is both a great writer and a great friend, read my earliest drafts and encouraged me to keep writing. Online writer friends provided support, too—my critique group and LJ pals, Verla's Blue Boards, and the Society of Children's Book Writers & Illustrators. I'd also like to thank illustrator Martha Gulley, along with Rob Igoe, Jr., Zach Steffen, & everyone at

Acknowledgments

North Country Books.

Most of all, I'd like to thank my family. My mother, artist Gail Smith Schirmer, created not one but two beautiful paintings of the *Spitfire*, the second of which graces the cover of this book now. She and my father read my earliest manuscript (about a shark when I was in second grade) and have supported my writing ever since. I want to thank Jake, a gifted writer himself, for being a supportive and honest critic; Ella, for making me laugh and reminding me daily what it means to be a spitfire; and Tom, for his love, support, and belief that anything is possible.

Chapter 1—Abigail

October 5, 1776

My palms burned. The waves tossed me about in the rowboat and threatened to tear the oars from my blistered hands. But I could see the dark lines of ships every time a swell lifted me high above the water. I could make out the figures of men moving about. They disappeared each time I lurched down again, into the belly of another wave, wondering if it would be the one that dashed the boat to pieces.

Again and again, though, I rose. Little by little, the men in the boats came into focus. The wind stung my eyes as I strained to see their faces. It had been five years since I'd seen Uncle Jeb, but I remembered the way his long, curly hair flew behind him in the wind, remembered the way his eyes crinkled when he smiled. It was hard to imagine a smile amid the tired and hungry faces I was beginning to see in the distance, but I knew he had to be there. I had to find him. He was family. He was all I had left.

The further I rowed from shore, the more fiercely the

wind blew. My brother's work shirt would have fit two of me; it flapped around my arms and ballooned out as the cold air blew down my neck. I laughed to myself for a moment, imagining this journey in the ruffled petticoats and embroidered silk bodice that Mrs. Dobbins insisted I wear in her fine household. She'd been horrified when my father delivered me, in a frayed, grass-stained dress and old shift on the day he left for Quebec.

I strained my eyes as another wave lifted me above the lake. Some of the men on board these ships were the same men who fought with Father and Nathan outside the walls of Quebec City. Perhaps some of them had even been there at Île aux Noix when the smallpox hit.

An enormous wave lifted my boat and dropped me, crashing again onto the cold, hard lake. The frigid splash of water soaked my clothes, and the coarse fabric of Nathan's knee britches clung around my legs. My frizzy red hair, impossible to tame, stuck to my temples and dripped down my neck, even though I'd hacked most of it off that morning in the barn. My cheeks were ruddy and smeared with dirt from the bank where I'd fallen, trying to push the borrowed rowboat off the shore. My clothes were worn and filthy. I was cold and exhausted, but I was pleased. No one would mistake me for a proper young lady.

Chapter 2—Pascal
October 5, 1776

I was supposed to be tending the cook fire, but precious little there was to cook. The general had written for supplies four days ago; it would be weeks before the fresh beef and rum and other provisions arrived. I gave the thick pea soup a stir and let my attention drift in the direction of the general's cabin.

I stepped over slumbering men, snoring under their wool blankets, and brushed past those on watch, making my way to the bow of the *Congress*. She was a row galley—a ship much larger than the galley where my stepfather and I had been placed when we first came. Still, there was little room to move about.

When I was near enough to hear the gruff voices within the cabin, I stopped and pretended to adjust a bundle of fascine—the sticks tied together to provide us some protection against musket fire from the island, where Indians fighting with the British fired from thick groves of trees. A high-pitched, cracking voice rang out over the sound of the wind and waves.

"If we stay here, we are trapped. At the very least, if we fight on the retreat on the broad lake, there shall be somewhere to run."

"This is where we shall wait," said another voice, stronger, more certain than the first.

"It is a plan for fools," argued the other man. "You've often complained to General Gates yourself. We are outmanned, outgunned. Our men have no experience and few supplies. To fight the British in this narrow channel is a death wish. They'll surround us, and we'll be trapped."

"Think you we'll fare any better taking this crew of landlubbers onto the broad lake? None of them know how to sail. If we go and the wind shifts, our gunboats will be standing still. We could row until we've worn out our oars and still find ourselves stuck in the middle of their strongest firing power. We stay!"

A loud thump startled me. As I walked away, the door to the cabin opened. A frazzled gunboat captain stalked out, his eyes burning with frustration. The other men remained. One stood at the center of the group, no taller than the rest, but stronger and sturdier looking, his black hair gathered at his neck, his fist still clenched where it had landed with a thud on the table.

"Now," said the man, unclenching his hand to pick up a quill pen. "When it is time, we shall assemble the ships thus."

I tried to inch closer to hear the plan, but the door swung shut, and I heard another of the ship's crew calling to me.

"Pascal! Yer pot's a-boilin' over, boy!"

As the youngest member of the crew, I did the jobs no one else wanted, squeezed into the places no one else fit. Just twelve years old, I was still small, able to retrieve things from the deeper crevices of the boat's cramped storage areas. My stepfather lied about my day of birth when we joined the crew. Though I wouldn't turn thirteen until October 12, he'd written that down as my age, lest he be denied the extra shillings he received for bringing me along to join the force.

I hurried back to the fire, where the pot of slushy, dull-green soup gurgled sickly over the sides of the cast iron pot. I lifted the lid and stirred with the wooden spoon I'd left nearby.

With the noon meal back under control, I stood at the railing and looked out toward the New York shore. The lake was churning, rough and wild. Watching the white-caps foam up and disappear, I thought I saw something else for a moment. A rowboat. It would appear on the crest of a wave only to be swallowed up again, but it was there. I don't know how long I watched it nearing our ship before I thought to tell someone. Any approaching vessel could mean a very real threat from an enemy; I should have reported it immediately. But by then, the figure rowing the boat had come into view. His rowboat was swamped, barely floating as it knocked against the side of our great row galley, tossed by the growling waves. The person rowing was a mere boy; he looked to be even younger than I was.

Chapter 3—Abigail
October 5, 1776

It didn't occur to me until the rowboat was nearly clunking into the sides of the great ship. What was I going to say to them? Certainly not the truth. "Hello, my name is Abigail Smith. I know you don't generally have young ladies as part of your fleet, but I just need to join you until I can find my uncle and perhaps accompany him home after the battle, so that I won't have to wear those blessed petticoats and practice embroidery anymore."

The absurdity of it struck me, and then and there, in the middle of the great, crashing lake in a leaky rowboat, I laughed. The boat tossed me from side to side as it lurched about on the waves. It was like riding in the hand of a clumsy giant. I should have been struggling for my life, but I stopped rowing, and I laughed. It was the first time since I'd heard the news of Papa and Nathan dying of smallpox as they camped with the wounded army after the raid on Quebec, the news that Mrs. Dobbins had told me in her tidy kitchen and followed with the admonition that ladies grieve quietly. For the first time now, I laughed.

I laughed so that tears streamed down my cheeks, numb though they were with the cold wind. It's a fine line between laughter and tears, my mother had told me once when I went with her to assist with a birth on the Jones farm nearby. The mother, a frail woman with exhausted eyes, had broken into a half-sob, half-smile, when her son was finally born.

"Is she laughing, Mama, or crying?" I remember asking.

"Tis just a quick breath that separates the two," Mama had answered. She had smiled and squeezed the woman's hand, and I knew enough not to ask more.

A giant wave sloshed over the side of the rowboat then, washing my face with frigid lake water. I raised a shoulder, trying in vain to dry my cheek with the damp cotton of my shirt. When I looked up, I saw that I had drifted much closer to the large boats, close enough to see a young boy squinting over the railing of one of them. He looked to be about Nathan's age.

I started rowing again, and with each pull of the oars, imagined what I would call up to the young man at the railing. The truth is best, Papa always said, if for no other reason than lies are too hard to remember. But the truth wouldn't work. The truth would have me ushered back to Mrs. Dobbins' sitting room quicker than the firing of a musket. I had abandoned truth hours ago, when I cut off my hair, dressed in my brother's clothes, and untied the rowboat with shaking hands.

I would tell some of it, I decided. I would tell them that I was an orphan, that my father and brother had died in the smallpox outbreak that decimated the Continental Army at Île aux Noix on its retreat from Quebec. I would tell them that I was seeking my uncle to see if he and his wife might take me in after the war. And I would tell them that for now, I wanted to help fight.

At that moment, I pulled back hard on the oars and felt a clunking jolt. My rowboat had knocked the side of the bigger boat I'd been watching. I looked up to see the face of the young man, who had never left the railing. He was indeed about Nathan's age, perhaps fourteen or fifteen—but his eyes held none of Nathan's warmth. His voice had a cold and suspicious edge.

"Who are you?" he called down, and in that moment, the truth was carried off on the stiff October wind.

Who was I? A girl for whom frills and manners were like an ill-fitting dress. A spitfire, Papa always called me. He told me that word was originally the nickname for a Spanish treasure ship that was especially well armed with great iron guns. Full of gold but spitting fire—that's our Abby, he'd say, shaking his head, but he always said it with love.

Who was I? An orphan now. A child with only one hope left, an uncle who was presumably among the sailors on this wild and bitter lake. And to find him, I had to become someone else.

"My name is Adam," I hollered back. "Adam Smith."

Chapter 4—Pascal
October 5, 1776

I'm sure I sounded cold, maybe even cruel. But at that moment, leaning over the railing, I cursed myself for not alerting the ship's officers sooner. The boy looked harmless enough, but there had already been attacks of this sort staged against the fleet—men promising to join our forces and then firing upon us in the next instant. I had been a fool to daydream while this lad rowed so close to the flagship of the fleet.

Just then, another crewman called me to help with the rigging, and I motioned him over.

"Jesus, Mary and Joseph!" he cried. "The boy's going to drown. Help him aboard!"

"What if he's a spy?" I blurted.

"For the love of God, he's a child! Bring him up. I'll see to it the general knows we've taken him aboard."

I tossed the boy a rope to tie off his rowboat and helped him climb onto the *Congress*. He was smaller than I thought. He looked scared but whispered his thanks.

"I couldn't hear your name over the waves," I told him.

"It's Adam. Adam Smith," the boy answered, almost defiantly. "Who are you?"

"Pascal," I told him. I was going to stop there, but he stared at me, waiting for more. Something about the look on Adam Smith's face, the question mark in his eyes or perhaps the pain in his brow, made me go on. "Pascal De Angelis. My stepfather and I arrived from Old Saybrook seven days ago; we answered General Arnold's call for seamen."

"My father told me I was too young to fight the British," Adam said, and I noticed he seemed to be sticking out his chest, trying to look bigger. "But my brother went with my father. He's two years—he was two years older than me—fifteen. How old are you?"

"Thirteen. Well…I'll be thirteen next week, and I've had experience sailing," I added quickly. "My stepfather owns a merchant vessel on Long Island Sound near Old Saybrook, where we live. I've sailed with him ever since we came."

"I've never sailed," Adam said. "Just worked the farm."

"Then why have you come?" I asked. I knew it was the question General Arnold would be asking him shortly.

"My father," Adam said. It was impossible to miss the stab of pain that flickered in his brown eyes.

"Your father is here?" I asked.

"My father is dead," he answered quietly. "Smallpox."

I nodded. News of the outbreaks had reached everyone in the Continental Army. "Was he at Île aux Noix?" I asked. I had heard many stories of the smallpox there. Stories that haunted me. Stories of men moaning and crying out with fever through the frigid nights. Stories of the huge blisters that made their skin peel off onto their blankets. I saw the sadness in Adam's face and knew before he answered that his father was one of the hundreds who never left Île aux Noix.

Adam nodded. "He was with Arnold. He and my brother died together there, after the attack on Quebec." His voice trailed off, and his eyes clouded over.

"He was going to tell me about the campaign up north. He told the most wonderful stories. We'd sit by the fire after supper, and he'd pull out his powder horn. It had the most amazing pictures etched in it. Maps of everywhere they'd been. Sketches of the forts so real it felt like you could walk through the door. I'd look at those pictures and listen to him tell stories, and it was just like I was there with him. He was going to tell me all about Quebec," Adam paused. He looked so young then, so much younger than thirteen. "He promised."

I didn't know what to say to him. I was older than that, beyond wishing for a father who would tell stories. I was a man now, regardless of my years on the calendar. I didn't cry for things I couldn't have back.

Still, I needed to tell him he wasn't alone.

"My father died on a ship two years ago," I said finally, "We were all on our way from Saint Eustacius in the Caribbean, to start a new life in New England.

Montreal

Quebec

Isle aux Noix

New York

Valcour
Island

Lake Champlain

Split
Rock

The Narrows

Arnold's Bay

Crown Point →

Ticonderoga →

Lake
George →

My father promised me we would have land here—acres and acres. Then he got sick." I noticed a knot in the rigging and turned to untangle it. They could make the lines weaker; the ropes might break.

"So how is it that you went to Old Saybrook?" Adam asked quietly.

"Captain Warner," I told him and felt my stomach tighten. "He took a shine to my mother after we buried my father at sea. She agreed to marry him, and so we never went to Connecticut. When General Arnold called for seamen, Captain Warner told my mother I was plenty old enough. He got an extra five shillings for bringing me along."

Something occurred to me then.

"I'm not sure you'll get paid," I told Adam. "Is that why you came? Does your mother need money?"

"My mother has no need for coins in heaven," the boy answered. His voice was flat. "She died of the fever three years ago."

Adam looked down at his scraped red hands. "She was a midwife," he went on, shaking his head. "She knew everything about healing. She had jars and jars of herbs that saved everyone. Everyone else."

Tears welled up in his eyes, and I knew he needed to be alone. Men didn't cry in front of one another.

"Wait here," I told him, looking away from his face. "The general will want to see you."

Chapter 5—Abigail

October 5, 1776

I bit my lower lip when he walked away, so hard that I could taste the blood. What was I doing? Presenting myself in tears was hardly the way to be accepted as a crewman. I wiped my eyes roughly with my shirtsleeve and took a breath.

When I opened my eyes, Pascal was back. I got a better look at him then. He looked more like Nathan than I had thought. His eyes were so dark they were almost black, yet they held a spark of kindness. It just wasn't easy to see.

"You said you came with your stepfather. Is he the general I'll be seeing?" I asked him. His laugh was mocking.

"He's no more a general than I am. His interest is in the gold—not the flag," Pascal scoffed. "He's commanding the *Trumbull*, where I was until I was called to assist with the general's move to the *Congress* here. She just arrived yesterday, and she's the new flagship. We've just begun moving papers and things over from the old flagship, the *Royal Savage*."

"But why…?" I began. I didn't know how to ask all the questions that danced in my head at once. I had heard Mr. Dobbins talking about ships in the bay, had heard him say that my uncle, Jeb Smith, was among the crewmen. I didn't know why the ships were here, though. Pascal sensed my thirst for information.

"The general's been waiting weeks for the row galleys to arrive from Skenesborough," he said. "He'd nearly given up hope that they'd be here before we engaged the enemy."

I must have looked surprised. Pascal nodded.

"General Arnold thinks the British are likely to come tomorrow or the next day," he added quietly.

"General Arnold?" It was a name I'd heard so often from my father. The man he had set out to follow into Quebec. The man he would have followed anywhere. Papa believed in General Arnold the way you believed in the sun coming up in the morning.

"General Benedict Arnold," Pascal answered, and for the first time, he smiled. "You'll meet him soon enough. No one joins the fleet without his approval. But you'll not go now. You'll get an earful if you approach him without an invitation."

"But I must speak with him at once!" I argued. Surely, General Arnold would be able to help me find Uncle Jeb.

"Have you not heard of anything that goes on?" Pascal looked incredulous. "We are at anchor tonight in a channel between Valcour Island and the New York shoreline. We're waiting—just waiting here—for the British to come fight us. Some who have sailing experience are fiercely against Arnold's plan to fight the British in this place; they fear we'll be trapped. And 'tis likely we will. But I heard General Arnold say that we've no chance of winning on the broad lake because so few of the men on board have experience on the water. He thinks our best chance at keeping the British from getting on South up the lake is staying here." He paused. "There's talk we may lose the whole fleet, though."

"What about us then?" I asked.

Pascal walked away without answering.

I stood and watched the turning of time on the ship—the stirring of pots of soup, the heaving of ropes, the bundling of sticks. I don't know how long it was before Pascal returned. He motioned for me to follow him. We passed a short, squatty man with greasy brown hair ducking out of the general's cabin.

"Watch your tongues, lads," he grimaced. "The general's madder than a nest of hornets. The crew that arrived yesterday brought more than the galleys. They had a letter from General Washington that held grim news from New York. The general thinks the troops need more backbone, and he's letting Washington know about it! Lord have mercy." He left us and hurried off. The cabin ahead of us was silent.

Even I had to duck slightly to step through the doorway. Inside, a single lantern burned in the corner, where a dark, sharp-featured man huddled over a table. I could hear the scratching of his quill and occasionally, his muttering.

"It appears to me our troops or officers are panic struck," he said, his voice growing louder along with the scratch of his quill, "Or why does a hundred thousand men fly before one quarter of their number?"

There was such passion in his voice. This was the man Papa followed, I thought.

"Could it be," Arnold muttered, then scratched something out. "No…Is it possible my countrymen can be callous to their wrongs? Or hesitate one moment, between slavery or death?" He shook his head and let out a long, raspy sigh.

"If the enemy do not make their appearance by the middle of this month, I have thought of returning to Button Mold Bay. We are prepared for them at all times, and if they attempt crossing the lake, I make no doubt of giving a good account of them."

Arnold looked up at the wooden beams above his head for a moment, as if there might be answers up there among the spider webs. He breathed out another small sigh and dipped his quill in the bottle once more.

"I am," he whispered, "Dear General, Your Affectionate B. Arnold."

With a final sigh, Arnold thrust the quill into the jar hard enough to snap it. When he whirled around, my brown eyes met his cold gray ones.

"A visitor, I see."

I couldn't speak. This man's features looked like they were made of dirty glass. Sharp, and cold. And yet, somehow, I relaxed as Arnold approached.

"I thank you for taking me aboard, sir," I began.

"I've done no such thing. What is your business with the fleet?" he interrupted. I felt his eyes pierce me. They were the color of the lake.

"I'm here...I'm here to fight," I said.

"Are you now?" Arnold did not move. I remembered the suspicion on Pascal's face earlier that afternoon and realized how foolish I'd been. There had been spies in the Continental troops. I needed to explain.

"My family is gone," I began, and I thought I saw the general wince. "My father was with you in Quebec, and my brother, too. They both died of smallpox at Île aux Noix, on the way home. At first, my father cared for Nathan and the other sick men at the camp, until he fell ill as well."

"And your mother?" Arnold asked softly.

"Three years ago. The fever." I looked down and blinked. How many times would I have to do this? I swallowed hard and looked up again.

"I'll help. I'm old enough. Older than Pascal." I looked over to see if Pascal was angry. He looked only a little annoyed.

"I don't think so," Arnold turned away.

"Sir," Pascal began. I interrupted him.

"I'm not leaving. I'm staying here to fight," I blurted.

The general turned back toward me, and something flickered in his eyes—was it admiration? It vanished before I could tell.

"You've fired a gun?" Arnold asked.

"Hunting with my father," I answered. It was true.

"We'd go out by the river when the farm chores were done. One day he came back to the farm with so many quail, my mother's eyes looked as if they were about to pop out of her head. He told her he couldn't help it— said they were jumpin' outta the fields like popcorn to greet him that day." I couldn't help but smile at the memory.

Arnold turned. "Zachariah," he said softly.

Papa must have told that quail story around a campfire on the road to Quebec. Arnold knew, and hearing him say Papa's name made my eyes burn again. I nodded.

"I'm staying."

"Come." Arnold turned and suddenly started out of his cabin. Pascal and I followed, scampering like shorebirds to keep up with the general's long gait.

When we reached my rowboat, still knocking against the side of the *Congress*, General Arnold addressed Pascal for the first time. "Your friend shall stay with us. Take him to the *Spitfire*. You shall both remain on board, as we are yet one hundred men short of those needed, and I believe the season will be ended before we see them." Arnold looked at me for a long moment. "Adam, is it?"

I nodded.

"Go then," he said, turning away.

Pascal had lifted his haversack and was already untying the batteau that would ferry us across the channel to the other gunboat. The *Spitfire*, Arnold had called it. Papa would chuckle at the coincidence if he were here. If only he were here.

I stepped into the boat and pushed off, but I couldn't help staring back at Benedict Arnold. The kind man who had whispered Papa's name in the cabin was gone. In his place stood a grim figure looking over the water, and his eyes seemed every bit as cold as the gray October waves.

Chapter 6—Pascal
October 5, 1776

Adam said not a word as we rowed to the *Spitfire*. If he was troubled at the notion that we could be in battle against the British any day, he didn't show it. His eyes held just a quiet sadness, and at the same time, a sort of mischief, I thought. It was the kind of sparkle that used to dance in my father's eyes when he was teasing Mama. But that was a long time ago.

As we approached the *Spitfire*, it was growing dark, but there was still enough light left to cast the silhouette of a crewman relieving himself over the side of the vessel. Adam's jaw dropped; he looked horrified, as if he'd never seen a man doing his necessaries before.

"Isn't there a privy?" he asked. I couldn't help laughing.

"A privy? Of course, and we'll eat our meal tonight on fine china. The cook and servants should be arriving from shore any minute to start preparing it. You fool! You've just signed up to spend your days aboard a fifty-foot-long boat, crammed together with forty-two other

pathetic sailors. We're lucky if there's a blanket to sleep under at night. There's your privy, lad!" I gestured over the side of the rowboat as we pulled up alongside the *Spitfire.*

The look on his face made me feel horrible. It was a mixture of hurt and anger and confusion. And still, he was staring up at the *Spitfire* with great concern. Was the boy just painfully shy? I tried to joke with him.

"Adam, my friend," I said, slapping him on the shoulder, "We'll get you your evening ration o' rum, and you'll be hanging over the rail with the lot of us. There's no modesty out on the water. We're brothers, after all."

He laughed then and laughed heartily. I don't know what he thought was so funny, but I was glad that the spark was back in his eyes as he helped me tie off the lines and we climbed on board the *Spitfire.* The men were just finishing their evening meal. I looked into the big pot on the cook fire to see if any remained. An inch or two of the same pea-green sludge had thickened in the bottom of the pot. I reached for my wooden bowl and passed it over to be filled.

Adam, I noticed, just watched. It occurred to me then, he had no provisions. He hadn't even carried a haversack when he rowed out to us that afternoon. All he had with him was the powder horn slung over his shoulder. It was finely carved on one side, I noticed, and I decided I would ask him about it. First, though, I handed him my bowl and spoon.

"Go ahead," I told him. "You've had a longer day

than I have." I hated the pea soup that Martin had made the past three days anyway. It was too thick and had a strange metallic taste to it, like the time I bit the inside of my cheek, and my cornbread had mixed with the iron tang of blood. Adam didn't seem to notice, or to mind anyway. He pushed huge spoonfuls of the green paste into his mouth.

"Nice work," I nodded toward the powder horn. "Yours?"

"My father's," he answered, swallowing, and looked down at the horn. He ran his thumb over an etched map that showed much of New England and Quebec. "He had it with him all through the wilderness, on the march to Quebec. I heard stories. Their shoes wore out on the way; they left tracks of blood and ran out of food. One of the officers brought Papa's horn to me after it was all over. He told me that Papa spent every night carving, and whistling, of all things. He said..." Adam paused and closed his eyes. "He said he'd need the pictures to remind him of the stories he had to tell when he came home."

With his hand still on the powder horn, Adam rose and walked to the railing of the ship, staring off in the darkness toward shore.

Chapter 7—Abigail

October 5, 1776

Finally, some of them went to sleep. Sleep on a God-forsaken boat was something difficult for me to imagine, but my eyes were heavy, too. Half the men were on watch; they had to remain awake and prepared to fight in case the enemy should appear. The others slept, it seemed, wherever they landed. I had to step over their snoring bodies to get to the stern of the boat, where things were quiet by then.

I had been in need of a privy for hours. In fact, I was already feeling the need to relieve myself when I had seen that man doing his business right into the lake. I'm sure Pascal thought I was a fool for making a big deal of it. Indeed, I was a fool. It hadn't occurred to me how difficult it would be to hide my gender on a boat where forty-four men lived, essentially, in a single room. Where they ate together, slept together, worked together, and, I now realized, relieved themselves together.

There was no privacy on the boat, save for a cramped storage area near the place where the cook fire burned during the day. It was too small for a man to sit up, but I knew I'd fit in the tiny space. I took the wooden bowl Pascal had loaned me and scrunched into the two-foot crawl space between the two decks. There, between a barrel of rum and crate of grapeshot, I used Pascal's supper bowl as my chamber pot.

There was no one nearby when I crawled back out and quietly emptied the bowl into the lake. I rinsed it out well, made a silent apology to Pascal, and set it back in its place. As I searched for an empty place to sit on the crowded deck, I stifled another laugh. The contents of the bowl hadn't been much worse, after all, than the soup that filled it earlier.

Under the threadbare woolen blanket I'd been given, I drifted into sleep. It was a different kind of sleep than I was used to, though. My eyes were closed, but I was so aware of the sounds of the men coughing and waves slapping the sides of the boat, the cold roughness of the great gun I leaned against, the even colder reality that I was far from any home I had ever known.

When dawn broke on the *Spitfire*, the first thing I noticed was that no one else was dressed like General Arnold. Lord knows I was used to dirt; it had been Mrs. Dobbins' chief complaint, that my attire was always too soiled to be ladylike. And I was used to seeing the farm hands in their work clothes—clothes with strong seams and worn-out patches. But here was a different picture—men wearing nothing but filthy, tattered rags.

Even Pascal looked different in the morning light.

Rougher. Quieter. Colder.

"She's startin' to boil," said a red-faced man, nudging the black iron kettle that hung over the small fire, enclosed in a rectangle of bricks in the forward cockpit. A spit was suspended between two sticks; something thick and light brown bubbled out from under its lid every now and then. It looked to be the same pea soup they'd served the night before.

The men were hungry. They gathered around the fire that cooked their meal, its light flickering in their blank eyes. I watched the flames for a while, too, but found myself sneaking glances at Pascal. Here was the one person with the fleet who was my age, who might be a friend, who might begin to understand how it felt to be alone and scared. His eyes were so dark they seemed almost bottomless, and his mouth rarely found a smile.

He reminded me of the rooster on our farm that had pecked so mercilessly at all of the chickens. The creature was always looking for a fight, it seemed, and always looked a little weary from the effort of it all—like it was trying to be tougher than it really was.

Pascal looked up and saw me staring. It didn't seem to bother him. Without speaking, he passed me a biscuit.

"Ship's bread," he said, and bit into a piece of his own.

I went to bite mine but had to try twice before my teeth got through. It was like biting into a piece of wood. The cornbread that Mama had taught me to make years ago always turned out so soft and crumbly and warm. I missed it. Even after Mama was gone, that cornbread tasted like home. This tasted like something else.

Everywhere I looked, men on board the *Spitfire* went about their tasks, but there was none of the whistling or joking I was used to. They walked about like the living dead; an exhausted glaze hung over their eyes.

"They've not had enough rest. It's like they're working in their sleep," I whispered to Pascal.

"You'd best learn to work in your sleep as well," he warned me, his eyes darting around like an animal worried about predators, "Unless you'd like a taste of the cat-o'-nine-tails, courtesy of the boatswain's mate." Pascal nodded toward the quarterdeck where the boatswain's mate stood, his eyes narrowed. His right hand held a whip made of nine pieces of rope. The ends had been dipped in tar to provide a harsher whipping. "Ananius Tubbs was cabbed twelve strokes on his naked buttocks for sleeping on his watch last week."

That day, I concentrated harder than I ever had in my life, to learn the drills and commands as we went through exercises. Pascal stood by me the whole afternoon, whispering instructions when I forgot, trying to spare me the pain of being corrected by the boatswain's mate instead.

I watched as one of the crewmen climbed the mast to adjust the rigging. It made me dizzy to see him balanced up there, clinging to the mast with his legs as the boat rocked in the waves. When he came back down, he stood next to the mast, his hand resting gently on the wood, as if it were kin to him. He didn't notice me at first, but when he saw me watching, he still didn't move.

"She's a living thing, you know…this ship," he nodded up at the rigging. "Think about it. The trees, the hemp for the ropes, the iron—all from the earth, like us. A boat like this moves and gives and changes with the weather. She has a personality, sure as you and me. She breathes in and out, leans over, rises and falls, just like your chest when you're asleep." He took a deep breath. "You need to get to know her, boy, if you're going to be with us. She'll listen to you then, and keep you safe."

I thought about what he said, as I listened to the wood creaking when the sun went down and the waves churned up later that night. Pascal and I were assigned to the first watch, which meant we would work through the first four hours of sleeping time. The blisters that formed on my hands when I was rowing out to meet the fleet had burst hours ago. My blood smeared the rope as I retied a line on the starboard side of the boat. I saw Pascal look at me and nod, ever so slightly. I knew then that I was fitting in, that I had begun to take on the deadened look of the weary sailors I had wondered at just hours before.

I settled into the routines of a seaman, running powder, pulling oars, mending leaks. As the hours turned into days, I turned into one of them.

Chapter 8—Pascal
October 10, 1776

At first light, I sat up to stretch. Adam was still sleeping next to me, slumped against a barrel of dried peas, his woolen blanket kicked aside. I tossed the blanket back over him and leaned back myself. It would still be another hour before morning gun crew drills began.

When the gunners practiced, I always stood nearby to watch. I loved it. The cold, black guns looked like gold to me. I'd run the powder cartridge, holding it carefully cupped in my hands, until I had to hand it over. I always paused as it was loaded, waiting for the sound I had grown to crave.

In the few weeks since Captain Warner and I arrived, I'd become a man. I'd grown up more on this lake than in all my years at home. I no longer cried about Father at night. There were no more dreams of him, and I no longer woke with my cheeks damp from crying. It was better this way. Things hurt less.

But there was a new feeling that had curled up in my chest like some furry caterpillar gone to sleep for the winter. It was a tightness, a heaviness, like the iron shot that blast out of the great guns. I couldn't say when it arrived, exactly, but it was there. The blast of the gun was the only thing that could jar it loose.

I loved to watch the men assigned to the gun crews, their swift, careful actions in response to the orders— the precise tapping of the powder into the barrel, the delicate lighting, the final gruff warning, "Fire in the hole!" And then the blast.

I remembered hearing it for the first time, feeling some of that bound up knot in my heart shake loose. One day before this all ends, I had decided, I'd fire one of the guns myself. One of the big ones. I'd kill a British officer, or even just a private. I'd make a name for myself, and my father would look down from heaven and smile. And perhaps then, this feeling I couldn't name would leave me.

I never told anyone about this, of course. Not really. I did mention to Captain Warner that I might like to join the gun crew. He threw back his head and spittle flew from between his front teeth as a laugh burst out.

"Fire the guns! Ha! I suppose you've a mind to man the nine pounder in the bow, too—why spend time on a wee swivel gun?"

"I could do it, you know," I told him, gritting my teeth.

"I doubt that very much, and regardless, you shan't have the chance to find out. There will never be a boy under sixteen on the gun crew."

"I'll have my chance," I insisted, and barely finished

the sentence before the captain cuffed me hard on the left side of my head.

"Watch your tongue, boy," he barked. "And know that the only way that'll happen is if you're the last one breathing on the vessel." He laughed again and strutted back to the quarterdeck, his boots clunking on the wooden planks.

"The last one breathing?" I whispered at his back. "Perhaps I shall be."

Chapter 9—Abigail
October 11, 1776

It was colder when the light reached my eyes the next morning. The wind blew hard, sloshing waves against the boat. The thin blanket I'd been issued was still tucked around me, though it did little to keep me warm. I leaned up on an elbow and looked around. The man whose name I had learned was James Blake was stirring the usual pot of greenish-brown mush over the fire. Alas, we were back to this. I'd thought that perhaps the large ship that arrived the night before, the *Washington*, would have brought provisions, so we'd be eating better today.

With creaks and groans, the men around me woke up, telling news of the night before. The row galley *Washington*, it turned out, had carried some new recruits, though not in the numbers General Arnold had requested.

Apparently, it had been a lively night. One of the new men, Philip Templeton, had taken too much rum. It dribbled down the neck of his loose work shirt, since he wore no waistcoat or neckerchief. He reeked of too much liquor and weeks without washing, and sobbed on the shoulder of another man for nearly an hour, moaning over how he missed his wife Betsy, before he fell silent and began to snore. Philip Templeton, it turned out, was then assigned to the *Spitfire*, one of the men reported. He gestured toward a corner, where the red-faced, drooling man still snored, though his blanket was tangled around his feet.

Overhead, geese flew up the lake, and to the east, the sun rose over the mountains like a big, ripe peach.

"Snow on the mountains," Pascal said, yawning. "All our practice may be for naught, you realize. You heard General Arnold composing his letter in the cabin, didn't you? He said if the enemy has not appeared by the middle of the month, we'll head back south."

The thought should have comforted me, but somehow it irritated me instead. I sat up and leaned against the wall planks; their roughness scratched my cheek. The sunlight caught a spider web stretched between two sticks in the fascine. I had helped to bind the bundles of branches together and hang them along the sides of the boat to protect the crew from musket fire. We'd take some of them down to make room for more guns when the fighting started, of course, but for now, they hung on the ship like armor. They reminded me of the King Arthur stories that Papa used to tell us. The Church didn't approve of such wild tales, of course. When Mama was still alive, she would click her tongue in disapproval. She'd listen all the same, though. We always caught

her, staring out of the window, while Papa spun his stories, and we were all transported—to a world of castles
and kings where things were good and fair and right.

It was the web that captured my attention that morning, though. The spider had stretched its home around
the outside of the boat as well, oblivious to the danger
of musket balls. The web quivered in the stiff wind. It
seemed perfect, but then I noticed some holes where
clever insects had escaped.

I was leaning closer to that web to look for the spider
when I heard the clunk of a small batteau being sloshed
into the side of the boat. The man struggling to stand in
the small rocking vessel was a messenger from the
Royal Savage. His breath came in raspy gasps, and his
face was red with exhaustion as we took his chapped
hands to help him aboard. By the time the batteau was
tied up, Captain Ulmer was at our side.

"Get him some rum!" the captain told Pascal.

The messenger gulped his ration of rum and sniffed
loudly before relating the news. The British fleet was
on its way—twenty-two gunboats, two schooners that
held sixteen guns each, two sloops, and one huge boat
with twenty-six guns, including six twenty-four-
pounders. There was also a monster—a fully rigged
ship with eighteen twelve-pounders—great guns that
would shoot twelve-pound balls of iron into the midst
of our fleet.

I had never seen a battle, but even I could imagine
what such power could do to the vessel on which we
stood. The captain must have known, too; I saw the

confidence drain from his face.

"They'll turn into the harbor as soon as they see we're here!" Captain Ulmer's eyes began darting around the ship, like he was hoping to see some different, experienced crew. But all he saw was us.

"The general has his own plan," the messenger said, gulping a second cup of rum. "He's sent out the schooners and row galleys to lead the British right into the channel."

"Lead them in?" Captain Ulmer's mouth hung open. "For God's sake!"

The messenger laughed a sour laugh. "Ye should have heard General Arnold bellow! 'Carlton the haughty,' he called the Governor of Canada, who's commanding the British fleet. General Arnold said Carlton is a coward who lacks the stomach for battle." The messenger tossed his empty cup onto the gunboat and puffed out his emaciated chest in imitation of Arnold.

"'Why, he's expecting that monstrous beast will frighten us to surrender,' Arnold said. 'We'll bring them in.' They've headed out already to fire off a few shots," the messenger concluded.

As the news sunk in, the men stood still, even after the messenger's boat had rowed off. Captain Ulmer began pacing the length of the boat, as if he were looking for a way off at the stern or bow. He glanced up and down the line of silent crewmen.

"Clear for action!" he shouted suddenly. "You, boy!" He pointed to me. "Spread the deck with sand!"

"Come on," Pascal gave me a shove and nodded his

head in the direction of the quarterdeck storage area. "Sand."

"Sand?" I was confused.

"Keeps it from getting slippery."

"Will the waves be so big they wash over the side?" I asked him.

"It's not waves he's concerned about." Pascal's mouth had tightened into a grim, straight line. I realized then what was more slippery than lake water. Blood. It would be coating the deck before the sun went down. It was our job to do something to keep the crew from slipping overboard. I dug my fingers into the burlap, tore open the bag, and let the sand spill out onto the deck.

Pascal collected the wool blankets from where the men had slept and began dipping them in the frigid lake water, one by one.

"For the love of God, Pascal! What are you doing?" I rushed over to him. "We have but forty blankets on this boat. They'll never dry before nightfall!"

"Captain's orders," Pascal answered without pausing. "They're to be soaked and placed over the powder magazines to protect them from sparks. A spark in the powder would mean an explosion that would blast the boat to splinters."

Pascal kept on working, amid the constant scurry of men moving guns, loading muskets, securing lines, readying boxes of grapeshot. I felt paralyzed and just stood still for a moment, barely noticing the bodies that bumped me roughly as the work went on.

Slowly, I began to see an image of what was probably

about to happen. Papa had once seen a powder magazine explode when a spark landed. He told Nathan and me little about the tremendous blast. I asked and asked and wanted to know more but was sent to bed. Too young, Papa said. It wasn't a story for ladies. Nathan filled me in the next day. Three men died in that explosion, their bodies thrown clear across the ship, several of their arms and legs littered across the deck.

I felt a hand clutch my arm and jumped.

"I see them." Pascal had stopped working. I looked up, and I was not alone. For a moment, forty-five men stopped where they were and stared to the south. Our five ships were back, and with company. Struggling with the ill wind, a British vessel was beginning to come around the point.

Chapter 10—Pascal

October 11, 1776

Things on board the *Spitfire* changed quickly when that first ship appeared. It seemed like every ten seconds someone bumped into me or jabbed an elbow in my side. There had been precious little space on the boat when the forty-five of us were just milling about and running exercises. I felt sure now that we were scrambling to prepare for battle, someone would be bumped right over the rail before the fighting even began.

As I tore open another bag of sand, I considered the plan I'd heard General Arnold discussing that day. It was a good one. At least I thought so, though I knew that General Waterbury and some of the others thought it foolish. To me, Arnold's idea of fighting at anchor made as much sense as anything else. He was being realistic. There was no way a fleet of flat-bottomed row boats would be a match for the King's navy on the broad lake.

The sand spilled from the bag as if it were keeping time in an hourglass. In a way, it was. I knew the fighting would begin soon. I looked around and saw that others were going about their own tasks with the same urgency I felt in my gut. They may have worn tattered clothes and walked in bare feet, but they were ready. We had all seen the fire in General Arnold's eyes. With our belief in him, the sparks kindled in our own hearts as well.

I thought I heard something then and held up the sack of sand. It sounded like musket fire coming from the island. I squinted at the rocky coast. I couldn't see anyone, but I'd heard there would be Indians on the island, fighting with the British.

Philip was next to me, retying fascine to the opposite side of the boat.

"Hold this side, lad," he said, pushing the bundle of sticks toward me and stepping nimbly up onto the railing to secure the knot on the other side.

I tried to hold the branches steady over my head as I heard the sound of the shots again.

"Musket fire?" I asked.

"It's begun," he answered, jumping back down with a thud. "From our Indian friends on the island." He nodded toward Valcour, but my attention was fixed on the fascine. I wondered how much protection it could possibly offer.

Then a sharp cry drew my attention away from the bundled sticks. It had come from the Valcour shoreline. When I turned and saw what happened, my stomach fell. The *Royal Savage* had run aground. She was tipped, her sails empty and snapping in the wind. I must have stood and stared for two minutes. We all did, I think, before Adam nudged me.

"They've asked us to ready the shot," he said. I knew

he must have seen the ship, but his voice still held the same determination, the same hope, it had earlier. Obviously, he didn't understand. I shook my head and pointed toward the *Royal Savage*. With the British gun-boats closing in, the crew of the helpless ship continued to load and fire grapeshot from their stranded vessel. I knew they couldn't last long, though.

"She was the best we had," I tried to explain, as I stared at our strongest vessel, stuck helplessly on the rocks. Adam blinked at the stranded ship.

"Gather your gun crew!" Captain Ulmer roared behind us. The men who had gathered with us at the railing scattered like ants. Adam disappeared with them, called off to gather rounds of grapeshot.

"Boy!" shouted Captain Ulmer. I turned and saw his eyes burning on me. "To the starboard swivel gun— they need a cartridge!"

"To the starboard swivel gun," I started to answer, repeating the order as I knew I should. Before all the words left my mouth, I had the powder cartridge cupped in my hands. I had learned long ago to be quick about such orders. I moved briskly but held the cartridge as gently as a baby bird. I held it just as I had been taught.

My heart pounded in my ears as I neared the gun crew, waiting for the time to hand over the cartridge. I was vaguely aware of the crews on other ships starting to fire, but somehow, even the deafening blasts of the great guns echoing off the Valcour cliffs faded into the background. I focused on the gun before me.

A gaunt looking man named Jebediah Hayes stood at

the swivel gun. He was wearing what had once been a white shirt and breeches—now stained a dull gray-brown. His brown tricorn hat was ripped in one corner. His eyes peered out from under it, wide and frightened, and they made me feel scared, too. I looked away.

"Thumbstall on," commanded another man whose name I didn't remember. Jebediah pressed a filthy thumb on top of the gun to seal the vent so no air would pass through.

"Attend the vent! Search the piece!"

Another thin man with straggly red hair reached for the worm—a wooden rod with a twisted piece of metal at the end. He stepped onto the rail and hoisted himself up to reach around to the gun's barrel. He shoved the twisted metal piece as deep as it would go and twisted it slowly as he brought it out. I saw what looked a bit of scorched linen fall to the water.

"Swab the piece!" came the next command, and without stepping down from the rail, the man replaced the worm and grabbed a long stick with a piece of wool wrapped around one end. He stretched over the rail to dip it into the lake and then plunged the wet cloth into the barrel.

I watched every move they made, still cupping the powder cartridge like a secret in my hands. There was such a rhythm, such a cold routine, to this business of firing balls of iron. It horrified and thrilled me, all at once.

There was a low thwooping sound as Jebediah pulled the cloth from the barrel. I woke from my trance. It was time.

"Advance the cartridge!"

I stepped forward and handed Jebediah the powder to place in the barrel. I knew that I should have stepped away then; my job was done. But I felt like the gun held me there—like I couldn't be released until its vibrations shook me free.

I looked up from the gun for a moment, almost surprised that the world had kept turning while we prepared to fire. The battle was underway in earnest. The British gunboats had dealt with the north wind better than we'd expected and had formed a line right in front of us. Their boats looked newer and stronger than ours.

It was too much to take in. I turned back to the swivel gun, where Jebediah and the other man had already rammed the cartridge down into the barrel and pierced it by inserting a pin through the vent on top. They poked a quill with powder through the vent, so that when they lit the linstock, the flame would be able to travel down to the cartridge.

"Make ready! And fire!"

"Fire in the hole!" Jebediah shouted and took a step back. I stayed close, and when the blast went off, I felt it boom through my chest and shake my heart. I took a deep breath and turned around to face the rest of the crew.

Nothing could have prepared me for what I saw. While my world shrunk to the size of a starboard swivel gun, chaos had erupted all around me. I could only lean over the railing and stare.

On every ship now, men were frantically running shot and shouting commands to fire the guns. Heavy iron balls tore through riggings and shot up explosions of cold spray from the lake.

Smoke, thicker than I had ever seen, clouded the sky. With every breath, I felt like I was getting less air and more of the thick, black haze.

When I turned away from the railing, my feet slipped out from under me. I landed hard on one knee and put my hands on the deck to steady myself. The sand scratched my palm, but there was another texture there, more troubling still. It was slippery, sticky. I didn't need to see the deep red color to know that it was blood.

It covered the deck, thickest in the forward cockpit. Clinging to the railing, I made my way there. The cook fire had been put out hours ago; with the amount of black powder being run about, a spark would have been disastrous. The tidy bricks that had enclosed the flames were scattered; the cast iron pot had tipped over, and a cold green slush mixed with the blood on deck.

I rushed to the railing, leaned over, and vomited.

Bitterness stung my throat, and tears stung my eyes. When I turned back, I saw a man huddled on the deck. He clutched his right arm, and his eyes had a vacant look. His head rested in Adam's lap.

Chapter 11—Abigail

October 11, 1776

Dear God, I saw it happen. The ship couldn't have been more than thirty yards from us when they fired. I didn't even know then what the shot was; I just knew there'd been an explosion of water and splintered wood. I dropped to my knees on the deck and covered my eyes. I don't know how long I stayed that way. It might have been seconds, or minutes. And then I heard his raspy crying.

It was Philip, from the night before. Philip, who had hung on his crewman's shoulder and sobbed. Philip, the man Betsy waited for at home. Blood gushed from his arm, seeping out between the fingers that held it.

"What was it?" I whispered to him, kneeling down.

His eyes struggled to focus, and I thought he recognized my voice. I stroked his hair, the way father used to stroke mine when I was fevered. His whisper came out raspy and pained.

"Grapeshot," he winced, then closed his eyes.

I had seen enough of my mother's midwifery before

she died to realize that blood loss was serious. I remembered how Mama's face would turn white when a woman's bleeding did not stop soon enough after her baby was born. I took in the area around Philip and knew that he had probably lost too much already.

Pascal came then. He looked like he wanted more than anything in the world to run away. We were on a ship, though. There was nowhere to go. He knelt next to me and stared at Philip's bleeding arm.

"He needs help," I said.

"For God's sake, Adam," Pascal snapped. "Look around you. We all need help!" He started to stand, but I grabbed his shirtsleeve and pulled him back down.

"Pascal," I stared hard into his panicked eyes, willing him to compose himself. "Philip is going to die. Soon, if we can't get him help. Is anyone on board trained in medicine?"

He took a deep breath and nodded. "But not here. The *Enterprise* is the hospital ship. We'll need permission from the captain to transport him there."

Pascal stood and went to find an officer. It didn't take long. Captain Ulmer was barreling toward him barking about more shot. Pascal scuttled along beside him, taking three steps to each of the captain's one.

"Please, sir!" he yelled. "Someone's down!"

The captain barely glanced at Philip's still body on the deck.

"Take him to the *Enterprise!*" He gestured toward the small rowboat tied alongside our boat, then paced quickly back to the stern.

Pascal looked at me.

"He must have meant for both of us to go," he urged. "I won't be able to lift him alone."

While Pascal untied the lines that held the rowboat, I ripped a piece from my shirt. I bent near Philip again and tied the strip of cloth firmly around his arm. A red stain immediately spread out from the wound, until the whole cloth was drenched. Philip's breathing came more slowly. We had to hurry.

"Ready?" Pascal was beside me again. He lifted Philip's legs while I tried to hold him gently under his arms. He must have weighed three times as much as the sick foal I had helped Father and Nathan with on the farm. I staggered under his weight.

Awkwardly, we swung Philip over the side of the ship and into the rowboat. His body made a grim thudding sound when he landed.

Pascal rowed while I held Philip's head. I kept whispering to him.

"It'll be okay," I told him. "We're takin' good care of you." I said the things I had heard my mother whisper to women giving birth, and I tried to use her same voice—the one that was gentle and comforting but still strong and sure. I never looked up. Not once in the whole trip. The sounds around me were frightening enough, and I needed to be brave. I had to take care of someone.

Chapter 12—Pascal

October 11, 1776

As soon as I rowed away from the *Spitfire*, I realized how exposed we were in the small batteau. There was no more fascine—no more armor—to protect us from musket fire. Nor were there swivel guns on board the small boat, for mounting any kind of defense. I couldn't believe I hadn't at least thought to bring a musket.

I looked at Adam with every stroke of the oars, hoping to catch his eye. Somehow, being with him felt safer, even in the middle of the battle. But he kept his eyes on Philip, talking to him and stroking his hair. Strangely enough, he reminded me of my mother.

Once, a round of grapeshot blasted out of a British gun straight for us. It sprayed the waves, and I closed my eyes, bracing for the impact of one of the balls of iron. All that came was a cold splash of lake water.

I was sure the water would freeze on my face in the cold October wind. The lake's surface, though, looked as if it might have been boiling, so numerous were the nine-pounders and grapeshot that broke into the waves as they passed through.

Except for the comforts Adam whispered to Philip, neither of us spoke in the ten minutes that it took to row from the *Spitfire* to the *Enterprise*. I ached to tell how afraid I was, but somehow, it felt like voicing my fears might give them the power to come true.

When we pulled up alongside the *Enterprise*, a ragged looking boy about our age leaned over the rail to help us up. His shirt, too, had once been white like ours. But in contrast to the dull brownish gray that colored our clothes now, his garments bore the scarlet stains of fresh blood. It was everywhere. I didn't even want to give him my hand to be helped aboard, until I remembered Philip, still passed out in the bottom of the rowboat. Together, the three of us lifted him onto the deck of the *Enterprise*.

"Ooh, he's a rough one," remarked the boy. I assumed he was the surgeon's assistant. "Bring 'im down then." I waited for the boy to offer his help. Instead, he turned and started down the steps. His feet left dark footprints on the deck.

Adam and I lifted Philip once again and eased him down the steps to the cabin. I don't know what I expected the hospital ship to be like. Of course, I knew there would be wounded men, men who were sick and hurting. I knew. But I wasn't ready for what I saw when we reached the bottom of the steps.

The room was curtained with the smell of blood, the smell of death. Around the perimeter were low wooden tables; on every one lay an injured sailor. Every one.

The place echoed with a haunting chorus of moans.

One of them was higher pitched than the rest. On the table nearest me was a boy about my age—his voice hadn't deepened yet. He held his stomach with both hands, and his eyes were closed.

"Over here!" The voice of the surgeon boomed out over the men's groans. I realized that I was still holding Philip's ankles. Adam and I followed the order and hoisted Philip onto a low wooden table that had just been cleared. It was still smeared with another sailor's blood. I eased Philip's body onto the planks.

"Stand by, lads!" barked the surgeon, as he placed two pails under the table. One was filled with water; the other was empty, but I could see from the stains that it had been catching blood all morning.

The surgeon wore an apron too stained to tell its original color. His damp brown hair was long and gathered at his neck, but tendrils had pulled loose and curled around his face. I was struck by his red, red face; it dripped with sweat, despite the chill that pervaded the cabin and the drafts of cold wind that snuck in through loose planks.

"Over there," the surgeon gestured back toward the stairs, and for a moment, I thought we would be allowed to leave. But then the surgeon held up his palm. He frowned, looking down at Philip, then in a single fluid motion tore the sleeve from the man's work shirt, exposing his wounded arm.

I felt myself flinch as Philip squirmed, and a low moan came from deep in his throat. Just below Philip's elbow began a mess of ripped tissue, gushing blood more furiously now that the cloth had been torn away. I should have turned away sooner, before I saw the bone sticking out from the wound.

I looked up the stairs toward the noon sun, imagining the cool, fresh air. I tried not to gag on the putrid smell of blood and infection that filled the cabin. I heard a sigh and turned back to the surgeon.

"It's as I feared," he said grimly. "Simon is otherwise occupied right now, tending the other men. You two will need to hold him down." He turned to the table that held his equipment and began gathering tools. "Here, give him these." The surgeon held out a mug half-full of rum and a musket ball.

Adam took them. I don't think he noticed that there were already teeth marks on the lead musket ball. I was sure he didn't understand.

"Come on," he nudged me. "We have to help."

"He means to remove the arm, Adam," I whispered in a weak voice. I squeezed my eyes closed, as if keeping them so would make the scene in front of me vanish. "He's going to amputate."

"Nevertheless, he needs our help," Adam said again. I opened my eyes and saw the same determination in Adam's face that I had seen before. He was right. We needed to help. I looked down at the table where Philip was stirring.

"Philip?" Adam whispered.

"Good lad," Philip barely whispered the words, taking breaths that grew ever more shallow.

"You're on the hospital ship now. It'll be all right," Adam went on, brushing aside hair from the older man's forehead. He held the rum to Philip's dry, caked lips and helped him drink. Philip looked at me then.

"They're takin' my arm, ain't they?" he whispered, after he had swallowed the last of the rum.

My voice stuck in my throat, but I couldn't lie.

"Yes, part of it, I think," I told him. "And then, then you'll be okay. You'll go home to Betsy. She'll see that you get well. Here…hold this musket ball between your teeth. It will help."

Tears filled Philip's eyes. When he saw the surgeon coming with the tools, he closed them again.

"Hold his arm out straight," the surgeon told us, and we did so, gently but firmly. The surgeon placed a tourniquet around Philip's upper arm, about four inches above his elbow. He turned the stick to tighten it. I watched as the leather band cut tighter into Philip's arm. The bleeding slowed and then stopped.

Adam and I kept holding Philip's arm. I was amazed that Adam never flinched, never seemed shaken. He looked away only once, when the surgeon grabbed a knife with a long, curved blade. We had both heard enough sailors' stories of amputations to know what was about to happen, to know that such a blade would slice quickly through skin and muscle, leaving only the bone. I looked away, too.

It must have happened quickly, because before I opened my eyes again, I heard a sound. I don't think it will ever leave me. It was like the sound of my stepfather's saw on the trees we cut clearing the land, but this sound was so different. It had sharper edges to it. I looked before I realized what I was doing, and saw the surgeon's sweaty face. He leaned over Philip huffing and puffing, working the saw on the bone of his arm. It's the last thing I remember of the hospital ship.

Chapter 13—Abigail
October 11, 1776

I kept saying it in my head, over and over, so that I could believe the words. "He's going to be all right. He's going to be all right." I said it so I could keep whispering to Philip, keep telling him that he would see his Betsy again.

I looked up at the ceiling when the amputation blade came out. I hadn't even been able to watch Papa butcher pigs back on the farm. I knew better than to watch while a man lost his arm. I stared at the grain of the wood in the ceiling beams and tried to block out the sounds of the surgery.

I nearly collapsed when the weight of a body slumped against me. I stepped back to brace myself and heard a thud as Pascal collapsed to the deck. He had fainted.

The surgeon didn't even glance down.

"More rum, Simon!" he called, still running the blade back and forth. I took a deep breath and looked back to Philip's arm. Slivers of bone fell away from it.

Simon, the boy who had helped us to board the

Enterprise, scurried over, seemingly immune to it all. He lifted Pascal back to his feet and tipped the flask of rum to his lips. Pascal coughed, blinked hard once, and resumed his job alongside the table without saying a word. His eyes were open now, but they stared blankly into the distance.

Thank God I wasn't looking when I heard the thump of the limb being tossed onto the wooden planks. I didn't need to look for my stomach to lurch.

"The tenaculum, Simon!" ordered the surgeon, holding out his hand impatiently. The boy gave him a curved needle attached to a wooden handle. He saw me watching and explained, "It's for drawing out the arteries—they must be tied off, and then the tourniquet can be removed."

I watched again now, with the kind of respect I'd always felt for my mother as she worked. So, too, was I impressed with all that this gruff doctor seemed to know about saving men's lives during a battle. Philip was completely passed out, but still breathing. I said a silent prayer that he would be okay.

"You'd best get back to your stations, boys," the surgeon sighed, glancing up at us after he finished with the tenaculum.

"Is it over?" I asked.

"We just need to seal the wound. Simon's bringing the tar."

"We'll be going," Pascal said quickly, taking my elbow and pulling me up the steps. I felt guilty for leaving Philip, but I was relieved. I had no desire to see what was left of his arm dipped in hot tar.

As we rowed away from the *Enterprise*, I looked around. This time, I had no Philip to focus on, no patient to draw my attention from the water that sprayed around us as shot flew everywhere. I couldn't speak and thought we'd row the whole way back without a word.

Pascal broke the silence. I saw him staring toward the southern tip of the island and heard a quick rasp as he drew in his breath.

"God help us," he whispered. We both stopped rowing.

Another British ship was coming into range—a ship that dwarfed all the others. She was ship-rigged, with three masts that towered over everything else in the harbor. She was twice the length of the gunboat to which we were returning. I didn't know much about such things, but I guessed she must have at least five times as many guns.

"She's just about in range," Pascal whispered. We both began rowing again, but I kept breaking our rhythm. I kept looking back at the enormous ship. Finally, I shook my head.

"We'll have to surrender, won't we?" I asked Pascal. "I mean…it would be impossible…"

Pascal looked hard at me, his black eyes burning with real fear.

"It won't happen," he said bluntly. "You've met General Arnold. He won't surrender. He'll die here with all of us before he'll strike the colors."

Chapter 14—Pascal

October 11, 1776

The massive British ship drawing closer should have occupied all my thoughts as we rowed the final yards back to the *Spitfire*. Still, I kept replaying the scene of Philip's amputation in my mind. I couldn't believe the nerve young Adam had shown on the *Enterprise*. Truly, I'd thought him a simple farm boy—one who'd have no sense for battle, no stomach for casualties of war. He had such a strange mix of strength and softness, the way he held my arm when I rose again after fainting at the surgeon's table. And he never breathed a word of it after.

When we tied up the rowboat and boarded the *Spitfire* again, I was shocked at the difference in the scene that lay before me. In just a few hours, everything had changed. Ezekiel, Jebediah, Joshua, and the others, who had been so high on rum and the thought of a quick victory, had fallen hard. They leaned against the blood-spattered railings, their faces pale and drained of spirit. Their eyes were unfocused, their faces streaked with black powder and red blood. Only Captain Ulmer's voice continued the war cry.

"Excellent, brave lads!" he shouted, taking long strides up and down the deck. "Load the guns again! Quickly! There'll be another drench of rum all around!" He continued pacing the length of the ship, shouting orders and patting shoulders. Back and forth he went.

He was wheeling around when a shot that sounded louder than all the rest rang out. A second later, the *Spitfire* lurched. I found myself thrown into a barrel of dried peas and landed hard on the deck. I saw the captain tumble into the railing, nearly falling himself.

"We're hit again!" came a shout from the foredeck.

"Again?" Adam whispered to me, incredulous. He crouched on the deck next to me, taking in the chaotic scene.

I heard a string of words then that would have made my mother faint. They spilled from the captain's mouth as he barreled back to the starboard swivel gun, pushed the gunner out of the way, and started shouting commands himself.

"Here, lads!" A rough hand clutched my arm. As I was dragged toward the stern of the boat, I saw that the first mate had grabbed not only me but Adam as well. When we reached the aft cockpit, he stopped short, so that Adam and I almost tripped over him. He lifted a rectangular wooden hatch from the deck and barked at us.

"We're taking on water—great amounts. Start bailing!"

"Yes, sir! Start bailing," I answered, nudging Adam. He still wasn't in the habit of repeating back the orders given to him.

"Yes, sir!" Adam responded, staring at the bucket that had been thrust into his hands. The first mate stormed back to the quarterdeck and began shouting to more of the crew.

I looked down at the splintered wooden bucket and felt frustrated. As terrifying as it was to be facing the massive ships of the British fleet, as much as I knew that bailing was important, I was angry. I hadn't joined the fleet, hadn't worked days to prove myself, so that I could empty out dirty buckets of stinking water into the lake.

The British Navy was right there. This was my chance to prove myself in the heat of battle. I wanted to fight. And there I was, dipping a leaky pail down an uncomfortably small hole, scurrying to the rail, and dumping the water, only to start all over again.

We bailed until the sun slipped behind the New York mountains, and still, the water seemed to creep higher.

A few times, I noticed Adam at the railing, standing with his empty bucket, staring out over the waters. It was almost as if he were looking for someone. When I asked who, he seemed startled. He never answered but returned to bailing.

Finally, he stood at the railing again and whispered, "There must be a good number of brave men down by now. I can't see who's still standing on the other vessels."

"You can't see anything," I reminded him. He seemed so upset, so concerned about the strangers on the other boats. I laid a hand on his shoulder. "It's growing dark. You'll see in the morning that most of them are all right."

Adam nodded the slightest bit and returned to his work. Even in the dimming light, I could see the tear that slid down his cheek into the bailing well. Quickly, he wiped his face and stretched his arm back down to fill another bucket. I said nothing and gave him the dignity of thinking I hadn't noticed. He would have done the same for me, I'm sure.

Chapter 15—Abigail
October 11, 1776

I don't know how long I knelt there, staring ridiculously down into the bailing well. It was the first time I'd cried since I'd joined the fleet. I don't think Pascal noticed. He seemed wrapped up in his own thoughts, as we all were that day.

How could I have told him? How could I have explained that my uncle was one of the strangers on those other boats? Perhaps, one of the men who was no longer standing. How could I have told him that the only thing I knew to believe in then might have vanished in the thick, gray smoke that hung over the water as the sun went down? And even if Uncle Jeb were all right, even if he were one of the men still standing, still adjusting sails and loading cartridges, how would I find him and explain to him what had happened? How would I explain to him what I had done?

When I finally lifted the bucket again, the absence of sound struck me more than any gunfire had that day. The lake had fallen silent in the dusk. It was as if the world had suddenly stopped, right at that moment, and everyone had frozen in place.

"It's dark." Pascal nodded toward the West. I could just make out the last purple haze on the horizon.

"We're through fighting for the night?" I asked. I guess I just hadn't thought far enough ahead to consider what would happen when the men could no longer see to load the powder and aim the guns.

"Keep bailing," Pascal whispered, as Captain Ulmer and the first mate stepped back onto the quarterdeck— the area of the ship reserved for officers. Normally, Pascal and I would never have dared to come this close. However, we were still doing the job we'd been ordered to do. And indeed, the water was still rising. We bailed, but quietly enough to overhear every word.

"Give the men more rum," said the captain.

"More, sir? I realize we were just provisioned, but perhaps it would be wise to…"

"To conserve?!" he laughed bitterly. "So the British officers can use it to toast one another over our watery graves tomorrow?"

The first officer stared down at the keg of rum.

"You saw that monster," the captain went on, flinging his arm out toward the lake, where the largest of the British vessels lurked as a huge, dark shadow in the dusk. "The only reason we've lasted the day is because it didn't arrive until a short while ago." He tossed his haversack with a clunk onto the planks.

"What now, sir?" asked the first mate timidly.

"We wait," the captain answered gruffly. "General

Arnold has called for a council of war. We'll meet on the *Congress*, and I suspect we'll hear our fate before long. Regardless," he gave the first mate a grim look, "there will be no need to conserve rum." He stomped off.

"What does he mean? And what's going to happen at the council of war?" I whispered urgently to Pascal.

"He means we'll surrender or die in the morning," Pascal answered without looking up. "And a council of war is where the commanding officers meet to plan—to figure out what to do next."

"What can we do?" I leaned into the well again, raised the bucket, and looked to the south. "The British ships have been lining up. It looks like they have a mind to block the channel. We'll be trapped."

"If we're still afloat, we will be." Pascal wiped his brow with a filthy sleeve. "Keep bailing." I did, but I also stole glances around the boat. Normally, the men would have dozed, waiting for someone to bring news. No one did. They slumped in torn clothes, sipping their flasks of rum, and watching the *Royal Savage* burn in the distance. When her crew had finally been forced to abandon ship, the British boarded her and set her afire. It was strangely beautiful, though not in any way that comforted me. The orange flames lit the rocky cliffs of the island with a gentle glow, but it failed to make the night seem any warmer.

Chapter 16—Pascal

October 11, 1776

I tried to keep my eyes on my task, as we bailed those long hours. I was afraid that if I looked up, Adam would see in an instant the fear that gripped my heart. I knew enough of warfare, enough of battle, to know what dire consequences we were in when the sun went down. Out of ammunition. Out of provisions. Two vessels lost, one of them still casting eerie flickers of light over the night as it burned.

How could I let Adam, the boy whose eyes always held a fire of hope, see that there was no hope left for our fleet? We were beaten down, and we were trapped in the bay. There was no way for us to turn our vessels and escape through the north end of the channel. Any southern escape route was blocked by a line of British ships that stretched from the island, nearly all the way to the New York shore.

Though the guns had fallen silent, a new sound was beginning to rise on the night air. There was hammering, as the British sailors worked to repair the damage we'd done to their ships in the fight. There were voices—confident voices. And there was haughty laughter. They knew it was over; all that remained would be for them to open fire at first light. We would surrender or be destroyed. General Arnold, we all knew by then, would not lower his flag. He would go down fighting, and as a result, so would we.

I looked at Adam, still bailing resolutely, still working like it would make a difference. I couldn't tell him. I went back to bailing myself.

When the messenger's rowboat pulled up to the *Spitifire* and knocked into it with a clunk, Adam and I both stopped working to listen. Captain Ulmer leaned over the side, speaking in hushed tones for what seemed like an eternity. When he finally stepped away from the rail, the boat was silent, except for the sound of his boots hitting the planks.

We all stared at him. Not a man on the boat breathed a word, but a strange ghost of hope hung in the night air like a mist. We all knew that the British blocked our only route of escape. We had seen, with painful eyes, how outmanned and outgunned we really were, now that the full British fleet was in position. Our aching arms told us how much bailing had been required, how many hits our vessels had taken at the water line. And yet, the men who led us somehow loomed larger than life.

In that moment, when Captain Ulmer turned on the quarterdeck to face us, we believed he might have the miracle it would take to survive.

"The general has a plan for our escape," Captain

Ulmer said quietly, almost whispering. I struggled with myself, not to believe too much, not to succumb to false hopes on a hopeless night. But then, I looked from one scruffy, filthy sailor to another and read my own feelings on each of their faces as well. They were deciding whether or not they dared to believe it was possible. One by one, they leaned forward, deciding yes, and they listened.

The captain unrolled a chart and motioned for Adam to hold it while he explained, "The British vessels are lined up between the island and the shoreline. The last ship is here." He tapped at a spot a few inches from the New York shore. "General Arnold says they're reckoning it's too shallow there for us to pass. He says they're mistaken."

Adam's hands trembled as he held the map. I looked past the captain at the shadows that were the British fleet. Were we actually going to try to sneak past them in the dark? I couldn't imagine getting away with it, but I listened.

"We'll prepare immediately," the captain said. "General Arnold has ordered that all the oars be wrapped in rags to muffle their sound. We need a stern lantern set up, covered on three sides so that it will only be visible to the vessel immediately behind it. We'll be rowing out single file in a quarter of an hour."

The orders were given, and we set to work, different men than we had been an hour before. There was a strange new energy in the air, as we greased rags and worked together to tie them around the oars.

Adam and I were set back to bailing, for the leaks had only grown worse. We weren't told to stop until the captain gave the order to lift the anchor.

The whole night was wrapped in fog. The British ships were more difficult to see, but I could still hear their sounds cutting through the darkness, the hammers pounding away on repairs, the men talking and laughing as they drank spirits and watched the *Royal Savage* burn in the distance.

I held my breath as we started to move.

N
wind

Valcour
Island

American
Fleet

Royal Savage

line of
British gunboats

American escape in the night

British Fleet anchored during night

British Fleet

British ships

Lake
Champlain

Chapter 17—Abigail
October 11, 1776

I was afraid to breathe. What if I sneezed? Or stumbled into something as I did so often? I huddled next to Pascal and listened to the quiet breathing of the men who manned the sweeps behind us.

It felt like we were sailing along on a ghost ship, so quiet were the oars doing their jobs. The *Spitfire* began moving slowly past the British line. I could feel Pascal's shoulder against mine as we crouched near the bailing well, waiting for the word to resume our work when we were safely past. He was scared, I knew. He tried so hard to hide it from me, to be brave like a man. But once, when he looked up from bailing, I saw it. The terrified face of a boy.

Without turning my head, I could see Captain Ulmer just ahead of me in the quarterdeck. He squinted off into the night, as if he could will the gunboat to move faster with the focus of his eyes.

Just barely, I could make out the light in the stern of the *Providence* ahead of us. It glowed like an exhausted firefly, worn down and flickering in the fog and dampness, but still lighting the way.

I looked hard at the faces of the men around us. There was no doubt; the fear that had filled the earlier part of the night was still there. Now, though, there was something else in the cool night air as well. It was unspoken. None of us dared to believe yet that the escape plan might work, that we might survive this battle. Perhaps we were afraid that speaking that small hope aloud would make it vanish, like a dream when you open your eyes in the morning. And so no one spoke of it, but it was there.

All through the night, I listened to the breathing of the men and the quiet swish of oars sweeping the water. It felt like time was standing still, but every time I looked back, the flames of the *Royal Savage* grew smaller. Every time I listened for the sound of the British hammers and rollicking, those sounds grew more subdued, swallowed up by night and distance. Finally, Captain Ulmer turned to us.

"You'd best get bailing again," he said quietly. He looked all around, as if he were expecting to see the British ships pulling up alongside us, as if he couldn't quite believe it himself.

We had escaped.

Chapter 18—Pascal
October 12, 1776

When the sun came up that next morning, I felt more alive than I had in weeks. Back in the channel, part of me had truly believed that we wouldn't find our way out, that we would die there, fighting the British.

The fact that I was here, still bailing buckets of lake water, watching the sun rise over the mountains, stirred something in me. Something that hadn't been there in a long time. Maybe not since Father died. I turned to Adam.

"It's my birthday, you know."

"Oh..." He didn't know what to say. Nor did I, it turned out. We'd been struggling so desperately, clinging so fiercely to life all those dark hours. It was hard to talk about something as trivial as a birthday. It was important, though. I'd made it. When the smoke was billowing and the wood splintering all around me yesterday, I had wondered if I would live to turn thirteen.

A flock of geese flew over and honked. Adam looked at me, and we laughed. I hadn't realized how happy I would be to see the dawn.

The island I knew as Schuyler came into view with the first light. We were surely close enough to reach it now, even if the ship went down.

Adam and I had been bailing all night, without more than ten minutes of rest. I never said anything, but I wondered how long the *Spitfire* would stay afloat. Despite our constant efforts, the water grew deeper. By the time the sun rose, the men were sloshing around in several inches of water as they hurried to make repairs. They fashioned whatever primitive plugs they could to fill the holes left by British shot. I saw one man hanging over the rail, hammering a chunk of wood into one of the holes, even as the water spilled in.

I was emptying a bucket over the rail when I heard the captain and first mate speaking on the quarterdeck. I slowed the water to a trickle and let it run out gradually, so I could listen.

"We're not saving her," the captain said, pacing across the narrow deck. "We've lost everything we can lose—the swivel guns, the waist guns, most of our remaining provisions—tossed over during the night. We might as well let her go now." He ran his hand over the wooden rail, as if it were the shoulder of a troubled friend. "The *Congress* is ready to receive our crew."

Adam joined me at the railing, but I held his arm, and he paused. We looked behind the *Spitfire* and saw Benedict Arnold on the quarterdeck of the *Congress*. He was waving his hands wildly, shouting something at his first mate. The wind stole his words away, but the fury in his eyes made me say a quick prayer of thanks that I was not on the receiving end of the explosion.

The *Spitfire* was sinking, even as the captain gave us the order to abandon her. We barely had time to gather our meager belongings before climbing on board the *Congress*.

By the time we were on our way again, the *Spitfire* was halfway under water. When we dropped anchor between Schuyler Island and the mainland, I looked back once more. All I could see was the top of her mast.

Adam and I spent the morning assisting with what seemed like an unending list of repairs on board the *Congress*. The ship had been hulled a dozen times, and her main mast was broken in two places. The moments we stopped to rest were few and far between, but when we did, I could hear a chorus of hammering, coming from all of the other vessels as well. Our fleet had escaped, but it was clearly in horrible condition.

"The mast is ready—as ready as we can make her for now," said a man climbing down from the main mast. He dropped the last four feet onto the deck with a thump. "Someone should tell the general and see when he wishes to sail."

"We'll go," Adam said, jumping up. Without waiting for an answer, he grabbed my arm and pulled me toward Arnold's cabin.

Arnold was huddled over a table, writing, just as he had been on the day I first brought Adam to him. It had been just days ago, but it seemed like a whole lifetime, in a way. The appearance of the general's uniform told

that story. He was every bit as filthy and stained as the rest of us.

I looked down at my own tattered clothes and realized the past few days had changed me as well. I had seen some of the most horrific sights of my life, heard the cries of men I'd shared bread with, watched them die, felt as if my own life hung in the balance. And for all of it, I felt strangely alive.

Chapter 19—Abigail
October 12, 1776

I stood in the cabin before him, brimming with questions that had eaten at me since I arrived. Here was the man who knew all the stories my father never got to tell me about Quebec. Here was the man who knew where my uncle was, if he was still alive. Here was the man who could answer all of Abigail Smith's questions. But to him, I wasn't Abigail. I was Adam. And Adam couldn't ask those questions.

Arnold didn't notice us, and my instincts told me not to interrupt him. I sat down on a step to wait. Pascal stood for a moment and then did the same. Arnold was mumbling again as he wrote.

"We suffered much for want of Seamen & Gunners. I was obliged myself to Point Most of the Guns on board the *Congress* which I believe did good execution." Arnold added a period to the sentence with a loud thump, then dipped his quill back into the ink.

So it was Arnold I had seen at the great gun. I closed my eyes and envisioned that imposing figure bent over the gun; in my mind, I heard the sound as the shot blasted into the hull of the enemy ship. It was good execution, indeed.

"As soon as our leaks are stopped," Arnold went on, "the whole fleet will make the utmost dispatch to Crown Point, where I beg you will send ammunition & your further orders for us. On the whole I think we have had a very fortunate escape, and have great reason to return, our humble, and hearty thanks to Almighty God for preserving and delivering so many of us from our more than savage enemies. I am, General, your affectionate B. Arnold." He signed his name with a flourish and sank back into his chair, as if pouring out all those words had deflated him. Then he noticed us.

"Mr. Smith, Mr. De Angelis," his eyes narrowed. "The repairs of which I speak need to be made sooner rather than later. Should you not be assisting rather than lounging on my step?"

We stood quickly. "Please, sir," I began, "We've been sent to tell you that the main mast is ready."

Without answering, Arnold stood and pulled out his pocket watch. He walked to the cabin window and peered out, then strode quickly back to the table to seal the letter he had been writing. He tipped the red candle over it until hot wax dripped down. Into it, he pressed the seal with his initials and held it for a moment before looking up again.

"Very well," he said finally. "You've delivered your news."

Pascal headed back up the steps, but I stood fast,

waiting for more. I couldn't help it. Arnold raised his eyebrows at my audacity. My eyes welled with tears, and I turned away in shame. What had I been imagining? That General Arnold would somehow, magically understand what I needed to know? That he would invite me to pull up a chair and visit for old times' sake? It had been a foolish thought—the commander of the fleet taking time to talk with an orphan child who had latched onto the Continental Army. I started back up the stairs, but his deep voice stopped me.

"Captain Ulmer says you've become quite a seaman."

I wiped my eyes quickly and turned.

"I thank you for giving me the chance, sir," I answered. Something about this fiery man in the filthy, expensive uniform drew me in, no matter how frightened I was. I stood, watching Arnold's face soften from something that resembled a sneer to a look that almost reminded me of my father. I knew I should leave. The general would need to check on the rest of the fleet, now that the *Congress* was ready. Something held me there, though, until I finally had to ask.

"Would you tell me about your time with Zachariah Smith?" I whispered. "He was my father, remember? He was with you in Quebec." My voice was hoarse. I hoped that my father had not told his commanding officer that Nathan was his only son.

General Arnold turned away and walked back to the table, setting down his letter once more. He regarded me curiously.

"Do you have a sister?" he asked.

"No, sir," the truth slipped out before I could consider why he had asked. He looked at me for a moment, then shook his head slightly, as if trying to sort out a jumbled thought.

"Sit down," he told me, motioning to the chair where he had been writing when we came down the steps.

I lowered myself into the chair but didn't come close to filling it up as Arnold did. I felt lost.

Arnold did not sit. He paced, as Captain Ulmer had done in the hours after the battle, before the escape plan was hatched.

"Your father," Arnold said quietly, "Zachariah, was with me when I was wounded in Quebec. It was just before the retreat. Montgomery was already down. Your father risked his life to save so many of us. He carried four wounded men off the battleground that day." He paused for a long moment, his arms folded, his eyes raised to the ceiling. "If I had been there with one of my own boys like your father was with Nathan, I'd have been so worried about his safety," he said, shaking his head. "I'm not at all sure I would have had the strength to do what your father did that day."

Arnold knelt down on the wooden planks and put his hand on my knee. "Your father assisted the surgeons with my leg after the battle, with all he knew from your mother's midwifery. But more than that, he talked with us all—told stories to the men in the hospital camp— stories so glorious you'd have thought we were the victors in the last battle." Arnold chuckled, but his voice broke at the same time.

"Your father," he looked up at me, "was a hero and a gentleman. I cursed the skies when I found out he had the smallpox. The Continental Army needed Zachariah Smith." Arnold rose quickly and turned away.

"So did we," I whispered.

He stood, and I sat, for the longest time. I didn't want to get up, didn't want to break the spell of memories he had cast. But it was time for the fleet to move on. I stood quietly and was starting for the steps when General Arnold spoke.

"Abigail," he said.

I froze. He knew. I cursed myself for being fool enough to ask about my father. He knew. I didn't dare turn around. I was sure he'd be furious, sure he'd put me ashore at the first opportunity. I turned but saw only his back.

"Abigail," he said quietly, still facing the window. "I could have sworn Zachariah told me he had a daughter named Abigail. A real spitfire, he said she was." General Arnold turned to face me. He squinted a little, like I was a puzzle he was trying to figure out. There was nothing I could say. We stood in the small cabin, staring at one another for what seemed like an eternity. Finally, he nodded at me.

"Must have been some other man who said that. You'd best return to your work...Adam." I turned quickly, but before I left the cabin, I was almost sure I'd seen a hint of a smile in his eyes.

Chapter 20—Pascal

October 12, 1776

I couldn't believe how long Adam was in there with the general. I went ashore with some of the other men. We had earned a short rest, we figured.

Two more gunboats were beyond saving, so the men cut holes in the planks and scuttled them, surrendering them to the lake. A handful of crew members were still working to repair the remaining boats as best they could. For the most part, though, it was a matter of waiting for the rest of the repairs to be done so we could leave. One of the members of the gun crew from the *Congress* built a fire on the flat rocks, and we all gathered around it. Some of the men dozed. Others talked about where they had been, where they hoped to go next, what they hoped they'd do in life, if the British didn't catch up with us.

I picked up a shard of rock and scratched at the surface of my powder horn absentmindedly. It didn't work very well. I'd lost the needle I had used earlier to etch in a few designs before the fighting started. My drawings were nothing fancy. Some of the older men carried horns that were works of art. Their whole life stories, it seemed, were scratched into the surfaces of the horns that carried the black powder for their muskets.

I kept trying to etch with the too-soft stone, and I tried to listen to the stories tossed about in the smoky air. My mind was with Adam, though, back on the *Congress*. I figured he'd gotten himself into trouble, asking the general too many of his questions. It was with relief that I saw him row to the shore of the island.

He stepped out of the boat before I could warn him about the slippery green plants that coated the rocks. With arms and legs flailing, he did an impossible balancing act before landing with a thud on the slimy rocks.

If it hurt, he didn't seem to care. I had to smile. He stood back up, and with the green slime coating the rear of his trousers, started toward the fire. His feet crunched along in the fallen leaves until he plopped down beside me and reached out to warm his hands.

"You had your audience with the general," I said, hoping he'd tell me everything that happened. Adam was quiet, though, thinking thoughts, it seemed, that he was not yet ready to share. I went back to my powder horn.

"What are you doing?" he asked me.

"Etching in the *Spitfire*. I want to remember her," I said, scratching at the horn with the rock. The lines were rough, not sharp and clear as they should have been. Without speaking, Adam reached into his haversack and pulled out a needle. It was a sewing needle, the kind my mother had used.

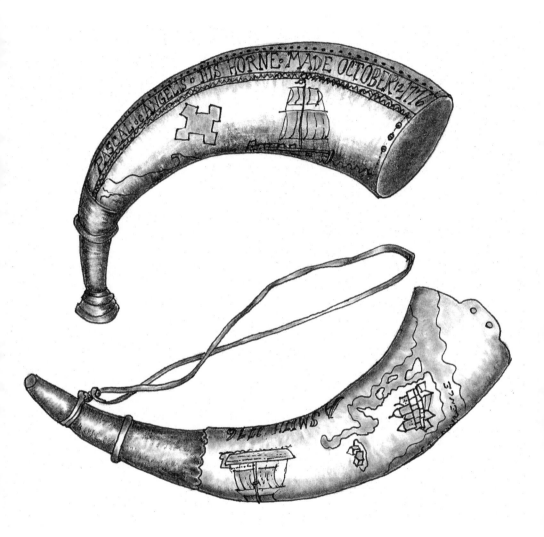

"Thanks," I told him. It worked a thousand times better than the stone, and as I scratched in the lines that made up the *Spitfire's* rigging, Adam leaned close to watch. He said nothing, and somehow, I was glad. The soft scratching sound the needle made was oddly comforting—so quiet, so peaceful in contrast to the booming echoes of the great guns. Below my hands, the lines of the gunboat's mast and sails appeared on the smooth curve of the horn.

I looked over at the powder horn Adam had carried since he arrived in his rowboat. Half of it was etched with ornate maps and drawings in perfect detail. The other half was smooth and perfect.

"Do you have another needle?" I asked him. He nodded. "You should add to yours, too."

Adam shook his head. "It's my father's horn," he said, closing his hand around it.

"You told me your father loved stories," I began cautiously. "He'd want you to tell the rest of his...and yours now, too."

Adam raised his eyes to the sky and stared for a long moment, as if he were checking with someone. Finally, he reached into his haversack, pulled out the other needle, and began to draw.

Chapter 21—Abigail
October 12, 1776

Pascal was right. It's funny how people just know things. He never knew Papa, but he knew what Papa would want. I was sure of it.

I held the needle to one of the smooth, blank spaces on Papa's horn. I hesitated for a moment, closed my eyes again. It felt right. I imagined the route that Papa and Nathan had taken, following Arnold through the wilderness to Quebec. Delicately, and so slowly—there was no room for clumsy fingers—I scratched the outline of our farmhouse into the horn's smooth surface. It looked all right.

I don't know how much time went by as I drew, as my fingers scratched out the scene in my mind. The farmhouse. The lake. The mountains. The border. And finally, the wall of Quebec.

Pascal looked over a couple times but kept to himself. Sometimes, friends don't have to say anything; this was one of those times. He just smiled and went back to his own work.

It was an amazing feeling, to draw those memories. With each one that came to life on the horn, warm thoughts flooded my mind. Visions I had locked away, because remembering hurt too much. Only they didn't hurt now. They made me feel a little sad, but mostly, they made me feel loved.

I ran my fingers over the image of the farmhouse, and it spoke to me, of the days when Mama and Papa first married and were given the plot of land. Papa had cleared it himself, and with Uncle Jeb's help, had cut the timbers to frame the small building where I was born.

And then there was the lake. I could hear the waves breaking onto the rocks of Schuyler Island, as they had broken at the mouth of the river two years ago, on the day Papa and Nathan and I launched that little boat we built in the barn. I picked up the needle to scratch a few more lines in the waves. The lake had been rough that day. I could almost hear Papa's booming laugh at the rollers that came over the side of that tiny boat as we hurried back to shore, soaking wet.

With my finger, I traced the route Papa and Nathan had taken from the farm through the wilderness to Quebec. Finally, I had a story to go with that picture. It's funny. I had tried to write those stories in my head before today, but they were always fuzzy and out of focus, the way the world looks on a foggy night. But as I ran my finger along the lake and over the border, I saw Papa in color, and heard his voice more clearly than I had since the day he left.

I saw that Pascal had stopped working and was leaning

over, watching.

"That isn't the end of the story, you know," he said, reaching over to run his finger over the etched letters that spelled out Quebec. "My father always told me that a powder horn's supposed to tell the whole story of its owner, like a book. You're the owner of this horn now, Adam. Seems to me your story ought to be here, too."

I leaned back on the flat rocks and closed my eyes. I felt the warmth of the fire on my left side, the warmth of the sun on my eyelids. I took a deep breath, and the smell of fallen leaves began to mix with the smell of black powder that had lingered most of the day.

I held the horn in my hands. Even with my eyes closed, I could see the designs as I traced them with my fingers. On one side of the horn was an empty, smooth area. Pascal was right again. It was my horn now, and my story. I sat up.

"Would you do the *Spitfire* for me, like yours?" I asked him.

Pascal nodded solemnly and took the horn. I moved closer to watch as he started to work.

The sun was no longer overhead when the sounds of hammering finally gave way to silence. The leaves left on the trees rustled as the wind picked up from the north.

"There," Pascal said quietly, handing the horn back to me. He had carved an image of the *Spitfire*, identical to the one on his own horn. Next to it was etched, "Battle of Lake Champlain—October 11, 1776."

I imagined the real *Spitfire*, resting silently on the bottom of the lake by now. "It's beautiful," I whispered, running my hand over the picture. I gave the horn back to Pascal. "You need to sign it," I said.

"No, it should have your name and today's date. See?" Pascal handed me his own horn, on which he had engraved, "Pascal De Angelis, His Horne Made October 12, 1776."

"I'll do that, too," I promised, "but sign yours here." I pointed to a spot next to the *Spitfire*. "We won't always be together, you know." He nodded thoughtfully, took the horn from my hand, and signed it.

I took the horn back and scratched in my name—A. Smith—in the space that remained. I had just finished when General Arnold's command cut through the waves and the crackling of the fire.

"Let's go, lads!" he boomed from the deck of the *Congress*. "The leaks are fixed and we must head south for Crown Point. We have reports the enemy has left the island and is in pursuit."

Pascal rose to his feet and offered me a hand. I stood but waved him to go on alone. I was on dry land for the first time in days and was not going to waste the opportunity to relieve myself without squatting in a spider-infested storage nook.

As Pascal headed for the rowboat, I climbed up the bank, through a thicket of bushes, and into a small clearing in the trees. I waited to unbutton my drawers until the sounds of the men's voices began to fade on the waves. I had rowed to the island alone and would take the same little boat back to the *Congress* when I was finished. With just one small person on board, I'd be quick; there would be no problem catching up.

I lowered my breeches, gathered Nathan's bulky work shirt around my waist, and squatted over the weeds. Just as I started to go, I heard a rustle of dry leaves. Before I could move, Pascal stepped into the clearing.

I dropped the shirt to cover myself and scrambled to pull up my breeches but ended up tumbling into a thorn bush that scratched my bottom like an angry cat. The more I struggled to untangle myself, the more stuck I got, until finally, with a great shrieking rip, I stood upright, half my shirt still tangled in the thorns and my pants still gathered around my ankles.

Pascal stood at the edge of the clearing, where he had frozen in place when he first saw me. His mouth hung open like he was trying to catch flies, and his eyes were the size of six-pound shot.

"You might look away!" I told him. My face flushed, and I reached down to pull up my breeches.

He didn't. And I knew he wasn't trying to be rude. He just couldn't believe what he had come upon in the trees. He closed his mouth and opened it again like he was about to say something. Nothing came out though. He blinked twice instead.

"Who are you?" he finally asked, when I had covered myself.

"Abigail," I said quietly. "Not Adam. Abigail. Other than that, I'm the same person you've known since I rowed out and you met me at the railing."

"You're a girl," Pascal replied, and his mouth hung

open again.

Perhaps I should have apologized. Perhaps I should have explained more or told him why I hadn't let him know sooner. But the right words for all that just wouldn't form themselves in my mind. In fact, all I could think of was how blessed funny he had looked coming through those bushes and seeing I was a girl.

So I laughed. He stared at me even harder for a minute, then shook his head and laughed too.

"Adam...Abigail," he began. "You are quite possibly the worst girl I've met in my life."

"Mrs. Dobbins would quite agree with you," I said, smiling. "But from you, I'll take it as a compliment." His face got serious then.

"They'll put you off the boat immediately if they find out, you know. What will you do?" he asked.

"I thought of that. Truth be told, I'm lucky it's taken this long for someone to figure it out. I need to find my Uncle Jeb. He's on the *Congress* now, General Arnold said. I need somehow for him to know that I'm here, that I need him, that I need a home when this is all over. I need..." I paused. "I think I need your help to talk with him, now that you know."

There was a call from out on the lake then, and we both remembered the fleet was about to depart. With thorns scraping our skin and clinging to our breeches, we tore through the bushes, jumped down the bank, and rushed for the rowboat. We just made it, climbing into the *Congress* as the anchor was lifted.

The sails of the British fleet were already visible. I

was turning to look for an officer, to see where I could be of assistance, when I walked right into the chest of a burly red-haired man.

"For the love of God, boy!" he boomed. "Watch your place! I'll not survive the British Navy to be bumped overboard by a wee lad!" His voice was deep and loud, but he smiled. He reached out with a huge, chapped hand and rubbed my work cap into my hair. Another man brushed by him.

"Hey, there," the other man laughed and clapped the red-haired man on the shoulder. "Don't scare the boy, Jeb!"

They both walked off toward the stern of the ship. I stared after them. I had just crashed headlong into my uncle. And he hadn't recognized me.

Chapter 22—Pascal

October 12, 1776

When the *Congress* lifted its anchor, I was assigned right away to man one of the sweeps—the long oars that would move us up the lake, toward safety at the fort. Normally, it was a job for larger men, but the crew was sparse. Some sixty men had been lost in the battle, and all of us who remained were put to work.

The rowing was difficult but it felt good. The job had a soothing, rhythmic cadence to it—two steps forward, oar in the water, pull...two steps back, out of the water, breathe...I fell into a pattern and drifted into my thoughts.

The same words played over in my mind. He was a girl. Adam, who had eaten with me and slept beside me, was a girl. Adam, who restrained a wounded man while his arm was cut off. Adam, who never said anything to anyone about the fact that I fainted during the surgery. Adam, who understood so perfectly what it was like to be a young man trying to prove yourself, wasn't a young man after all.

And yet, at the same time, he…she…Abigail was still my friend. I told him…her…well, him at the time, things I hadn't told anyone. I didn't know how to feel, except confused. I decided to concentrate on the sound of the oars sweeping the water.

When I did that, the image of him…no, definitely her…squatting in the clearing popped into my mind. I shook my head and chased it away. To picture a young woman unclothed was a sin, I knew. But she appeared in my mind again, this time with her head thrown back in laughter. Confused or otherwise, I had to smile. She really did make a better boy than a girl. And she was a fine friend—one who had taught me more about how to be a man than any man I'd ever known. I had to find a way to help her.

The sun turned the sky purple and pink as we pulled farther away from the island. Adam—I still thought of her as Adam—was set to rowing when one of the other men grew weary. I almost said something to the officer who ordered her to man the sweep. It was hard work, and I wasn't sure she'd be able to control the huge, heavy oar. I was wrong. She rowed quite well, and in fact, managed to catch my elbow once when I stumbled against a barrel of rum that was in my way.

The colors of the sky turned to a hazy blue and finally black, and we rowed through it all. There was a comfort in the repetitiveness of it—the way the sweeps moved in harmony with one another. The way we all stepped forward together and then pulled back on the long wooden handles, together, with one purpose.

Arnold came by from time to time, offering encouragement, telling us how brave we were, and promising a good meal when we arrived at Crown Point. It was the first I'd thought of food, and I realized I was hungry. We hadn't eaten since the morning before the battle, and even then, most of us had to leave our bowls half full when the order came to clear for action.

After every walk through our crew, Arnold would settle in at the stern, looking to the north. Even in the blackness, we could see the British fleet was getting closer. The wind had died down to almost nothing. Though our sails still filled from time to time, the *Congress* was barely moving.

Arnold turned to watch us rowing. His eyes betrayed his frustration. Clearly, every sailor manning the sweeps was giving all that he had, and yet it simply was not going to be enough. I willed myself to pull harder, to ignore the bloody cracks in my palms and make us go faster.

I looked to the north, where Arnold's eyes were focused. Already, the lanterns in the British ships seemed brighter. They were closer.

There was no chance we'd reach Crown Point before the enemy ships reached us.

Chapter 23—Abigail
October 12, 1776

Pascal had said very little to me since we got back to the *Congress*. Truly, no one had time to say much of anything. We were all set to our tasks quickly, and I was grateful. For the first time, I was assigned to row.

It felt incredible to control one of the twelve-foot oars that propelled the boat forward to the south. With every stroke, I felt stronger, and with every stroke, a belief grew inside me. I was going to make it.

I would survive this adventure as Adam Smith, and I would get to be Abigail Smith again. Not Abigail Smith, the girl who crafted dainty embroideries on her handkerchiefs. I was going to be Abby, who worked hard to do whatever job needed to be done, helped out however she could, rose to the occasion when someone needed her, and relieved herself in the forest when the need arose. And I was going to live in a place where people were okay with that. I was sure things would work out with Uncle Jeb.

For the time being, though, I was going to row,

because our lives depended on moving south. Even with my lack of experience on a boat, I could see that the British ships were faster than we were. They were gaining ground, even as we struggled with the wind. I tried to row harder.

My mind only drifted once in a while. Every time Arnold came by to pat us on our shoulders, I'd hold my breath. His big hand would rest on me for only a moment, but somehow, that kept me going. It had been so long since I'd felt Papa's hand there; just to have someone touch me felt good. Especially if it was General Arnold—the man who pointed the guns on the *Congress* himself, who led us past an impossible blockade to safety, who continued to build us up, believing against all odds that somehow, things would be okay.

Every time I felt Arnold's hand on my shoulder, I believed it too.

Chapter 24—Pascal

October 13, 1776

By the time dawn broke, there was no question at all. The realization had settled in the eyes of the men like dominoes falling. Those who had seen the most military service—fighting the French before this—knew it first. Their eyes grew dull, their motions about the boat less spirited. Next, it was the older men who'd been with the Continental Army from the start. Then finally, that deadened expression spread to those of us who had just signed up, answering the call for seamen a few short weeks ago.

It was impossible to imagine a safe escape. In the lightening day, we saw how much larger the British sails had grown overnight, how the north wind filled them, moved them forward so quickly, compared to the feeble progress of our leaking, battered fleet. Several of our boats lagged behind; it seemed certain we would be forced to engage the British again at any moment.

The British guns started firing again, as if to answer my thought. Our slowest vessels were already under seige.

A messenger from the other row galley, the *Washington*, rowed through the hail of grapeshot to speak with General Arnold. His eyes were round, his face red and shining, as I took his sweaty hand to help him board the *Congress*. He was fat, with a gut that hung out the bottom of his tattered shirt, over his pants, and he strained to pull himself up to the ship's deck.

"Message for General Arnold, from General Waterbury," he said, between gasps for air.

General Arnold stepped up to the man. I stepped back and squatted down to tend an injured man who was moaning on deck nearby. There, I could still hear their conversation.

"Sir," began the messenger, his eyes blinking madly, as if to fend off any anger his message was about to provoke. "General Waterbury sends me with a request to abandon his ship."

"No!" Arnold shouted, wheeling around to leave.

"But sir, there is more," the messenger said, shifting his weight from side to side. "I'm requested to tell you that the *Washington* is surrounded, sir. She's taking on water and is in great need of assistance. General Waterbury requests that you slow down to aid him. Otherwise, he wishes to run her aground and blow her up before she's captured."

"No!" Arnold said again, and stood with his feet apart and arms crossed, as if daring the messenger to add anything more.

"Sir?" The messenger's puffy face had gone from

red to pale white. "Are there any further orders then?" he asked weakly.

"Tell General Waterbury to push forward. We'll draw the fleet into a line and he'll have his assistance. He is not to strike his colors! Make that clear when you return. And do so now!" Arnold ordered, his boots clunking angrily on the deck as he strode away.

I watched the messenger return to his boat and begin to row toward the *Washington*. Before he made it halfway, there was a thundering of great guns up the lake—then a sudden silence. I squinted toward the *Washington* and saw why. The flag was gone. Waterbury had already surrendered.

"Blast him!" thundered Arnold, wheeling around and heading back to his cabin. His intensity scared me. I looked around at the other crew members. Wide-eyed, they were working furiously. The gut feeling I'd shared with Adam—Abigail—was right. Arnold would never surrender.

The British ships sailed on past the *Washington*. They were almost within firing range.

This time, I knew, we would not drop anchor to fire the guns. We would fight on the retreat, hoping to survive long enough to make it to Crown Point and some help. As the British ships loomed larger, I couldn't imagine how we could escape a second time.

Within fifteen minutes of the *Washington's* surrender, the British had caught up to us on the *Congress*. Two British ships pulled alongside us, so close I could see the faces of the gun crews. Even amid the chaos, I couldn't help but notice their faces. They looked exactly like the faces of the men standing at our guns, tired and worn, hurt and scared. One of them looked like he was my age, maybe a couple years older.

That British boy in his red uniform met my eyes then. I don't know what I'd expected. Perhaps I thought they'd wear cold sneers and have eyes like stones. This boy looked terrified and strangely stunned—like he couldn't believe what was happening, couldn't imagine how he had gone from working in the fields to this.

"Pascal De Angelis!" bellowed General Arnold, and I jumped around to face him. "Lieutenant Goldsmith is down! Go man the starboard swivel gun!"

Arnold blew past, shoving me roughly into position next to the gun. A round of grapeshot blasted into the *Congress* at that moment, along with what must have been at least a 12-pounder. I tumbled against the railing as the deck shook.

"For the love of God! Get up, child!" barked the officer in charge of the gun crew. He grabbed my arm roughly and yanked me to my feet. His red hair had been gathered in back at one point but flew out wildly now, tangled with a scraggly red and gray beard.

"We're down to the boys, are we?" he asked bitterly, spit flying from a huge gap between his front teeth. "Well, speak, lad! Do you know the bloody commands at least?"

My eyes burned. "I have yet to hear a command. When I do, I shall follow it," I told him fiercely.

The officer's eyes narrowed. "The gun's ready for a

cartridge," he said evenly. "Lieutenant Goldsmith had just finished swabbing the piece when he was hit. You'll need that," he said, pointing to a spot on the deck. I looked down. The lieutenant lay on the deck unconscious, blood pouring from a wound in his leg. It had soaked through the sponge next to him.

My stomach lurched, but I said nothing. I picked up the sponge by its long wooden handle and set it back where it belonged. I locked eyes with the officer again.

"Advance the cartridge," he called to another boy, who came forward with the powder cupped in his hands. My heart jumped. It was Abigail. She met my eyes for a brief moment, and I saw the horror in hers.

"Place the cartridge in the barrel!" barked the officer. I leaned over the rail to place the cartridge and a handful of small round shot into the gun's barrel.

"Ram the cartridge!"

I stretched as far as I could, but my arms weren't long enough to reach around to the barrel of the swivel gun with the ramrod. I had to climb up onto the railing, balancing on one knee, to lean out over the water and push the rod into the barrel. Another shot hit the *Congress* at that moment. The ship buckled and threatened to throw me off like a wild horse. I clung onto the railing to keep from tumbling into the water. I lost my grip on the ramrod, and it dropped into the lake.

"That will come out of your pay should we ever see any pay, you idiot!" thundered the officer. His face was so red I thought he might explode.

"Prick and prime!" With each word, more spit flew

from his mouth. I felt a drop land near my upper lip. I ignored it; my hands were busy piercing the cartridge through the tiny vent hole at the top of the gun.

"Make ready!" boomed the officer, "and fire!"

I lifted the linstock—the long tool that held the slowmatch—and moved it closer to the fuse. My heart was pounding so loudly I was sure it would drown out the sound of the battle.

This was the moment I had imagined since I first joined the fleet. The gun was aimed at the ship alongside us—not fifty feet away. I held the slowmatch to the fuse and shouted, "Fire in the hole!"

I listened with a strange curiosity to the sound of my own voice. The words that flew from my mouth sounded like they belonged to someone else—someone older and harder. Someone colder.

The blast of the gun knocked me off my feet, but I jumped up from the deck and leaned forward over the rail, straining to see through the smoke where the shot had gone, what damage had been done. It was impossible to tell. Had I even hit anyone? The air was full of smoke, full of the sounds and smells of death. It came from every direction, impossible to pinpoint.

I felt my chest tighten. I thought it would be different, this moment. I had expected so much more and felt so frustrated then that I wanted to scream. I wanted to pound the officer with the unruly red hair and spit back at him.

I slumped against the railing and looked again to the enemy ship alongside us. And then I saw. Two men were lifting a third—a small figure—from the deck. His thigh was torn to pieces, and even over the gunfire, I could hear his scream. I recognized it not as a man's scream, but as the cry of a boy—the boy whose frightened eyes had met mine less than a quarter of an hour ago.

There it was. The answer I'd wanted. I had hit my mark.

Chapter 25—Abigail

October 13, 1776

I never moved after I gave him the cartridge. It was too terrible to watch, and too terrible to turn away. It felt like one of the nightmares I had after Papa and Nathan left. I'd lie in the cold, frilly bed in Mrs. Dobbins' spare room and dream of hiding from British soldiers. If I stayed still enough in those dreams, if I was quiet and proper enough, and fit in, they didn't find me. Perhaps I hoped that if I stood quietly enough on that hellish deck, it would turn from a horrid reality back to a dream.

Pascal made it real again. I felt his hand clutch my arm as he dropped to his knees sobbing.

"What bloody day is this?" he choked, oblivious to the sneer of the officer who loomed above us. "Who am I?"

What could I answer? Indeed, who was I? The girl who wore a boy's clothes to fight as a man and ultimately, couldn't handle the reality of her choice... couldn't do it any better than she could become a lady back home.

My hand was smeared with the blood of the lieutenant who lay moaning three feet away on the deck. It didn't matter. Not here. Not now. I rested my hand on Pascal's matted black hair and let go of the tears I'd been blinking back for so long.

The lieutenant let out another moan, more shuddering, more pained. Pascal pulled away from me to kneel by him, and I followed.

The injured man's hand rested limply on the blood-stained deck, but his eyes focused on me. I reached for my flask and poured a few drops of rum into his mouth. He coughed and grimaced. He looked weak. He had probably lost too much blood already.

"Can I help, sir?" I whispered to him. He said nothing, and at first I thought he didn't hear me over the great guns whose booms still echoed off the cliffs on shore.

"Sir," the man whispered back, staring up at the sky. "I think that you might call me James now, for at this point, I am no longer acting as an officer in this battle." He paused. "Nor shall I act as an officer again, I suspect." He closed his eyes.

Pascal looked at me, then reached for the lieutenant's hand.

"James," he said, "when we arrive at Crown Point, there will be medical care. The *Enterprise* is probably there already. As soon as we catch up, they'll help you."

"What is your name, lad?" the man asked, looking up.

"Pascal," he said and looked at me. "And this is…" he paused and looked hard at my face. "This is my friend," he finished quietly.

"Pascal and…" James Goldsmith looked up at me and squinted, a question in his hurting eyes.

"Adam," I said quickly.

"And Adam," he went on. "I am not so wholly injured that I do not see and hear what goes on around me. I'll not see Crown Point this night, or ever again. 'Tis likely none of us will."

His words hit me like a blow to the chest. I had been thinking that the lieutenant would probably pass on soon, but somehow, in all the chaos, I hadn't stopped to think of what losing the battle would mean for the rest of us. For Pascal. For Uncle Jeb. For me.

"Do you believe in heaven, lads?" James whispered, his eyes closed again.

"Yes," Pascal said, almost too quickly. "I…Mother always told me it was so."

"I suppose I do, too," I answered. Another blow shook our vessel, and Lieutenant Goldsmith winced.

The truth was, I used to believe in heaven. I clung to the idea and imagined its every detail after Mama died. It brought me such comfort to think of her someplace warm and safe and good. I was sure there was a God, sure that He was taking good care of Mama up there on a cloud.

But that seemed like a childish notion now. The truth was, I hadn't prayed since the day I heard about Papa and Nathan. I'd knelt by my bed each night as was expected, and I'd worn my good dresses to church with the Dobbins family. But every time I tried to pray, the words just didn't come. It seemed like a lie somehow.

Now, though, looking down at James, I wondered. There must be something else, I thought, some other side to this darkness.

"What do you suppose it's like there?" James asked.

I was surprised to hear Pascal answer.

"My mother told me it's different for everyone—the most amazing thing you could imagine, with everything and everyone you love, and you never lose them again. She said we'll see Father there…" His voice broke on his last word, and James opened his eyes.

"I believe it's like that—and more," he said. "I think when you go to heaven, you get to see how it all fits together."

"How what fits together?" I asked.

"Everything." James smiled a little, but his voice grew quieter and raspier with every breath. "You get to see the big picture—and understand things we can't understand here on earth. Things like this…" His eyes drifted to the ships, still firing broadsides. He looked back at us. "This means something, you know. Even if we all die here today, there'll be a reason for it. Maybe these are the moments that will make liberty real some day."

"Perhaps you're right," Pascal said quietly, staring off into the smoke. "Even as it feels like we're tearing things to pieces, perhaps we're building something."

"Or maybe there's some other reason we can't even imagine. In heaven, I'll finally understand. I'll see my boys grow into men. I'll see my own mama and papa again, and they'll hold me like I'm a boy myself." He sighed, squeezed my hand, and closed his eyes.

Gently, I let go of his hand and set it on the deck. I looked at him a long while, before Pascal took my elbow and helped me stand. I realized then how long we had been away from the battle. Our ships had been running the whole time; we were heading straight for a small bay on the eastern shore.

I looked around and tried to see where General Arnold was. I couldn't catch a glimpse of him. What I could see were more British ships firing on us. The one alongside us still pounded us with rounds of grapeshot, and now there were two more enemy vessels at our stern, firing larger shot that had completely tattered our rigging.

Another sailor rushed by, and I grabbed his arm to stop him.

"What's happening?" I asked. "Where is General Arnold?"

"We're running into the bay!" the man answered, pulling loose from my grip. "The general says he'll destroy the whole bloody fleet before he gives up another boat to those savages."

I wanted to follow the man to ask more, but Pascal grabbed my arm and pulled me toward the bow of the ship.

"He aims to have us escape by foot!" he shouted above the firing. "'Tis a shallow bay. We'll need to jump!"

"Have mercy! Another one!" A voice boomed above us, and then a great figure appeared. It was General Arnold, and he was staring down at Lieutenant Goldsmith.

"Hang on, James," Arnold said to him. He put one

rough hand on my shoulder and the other on Pascal's and pushed us toward the starboard rail. "Go on, lads," he ordered in a voice that was weary but somehow still strong. "We're going ashore here—destroying the fleet and heading out on foot. Someone will come for him," he promised, nodding down at James. Then he disappeared into the swarm of men.

"Leave the colors flying! The ships will go down ours, at least!" I heard him shout as he moved on.

Suddenly, the ship lurched; I knew it must have run aground. And so, too, I knew it was time. All around us, men rushed back and forth; some had already started abandoning the ship to run ashore. All the while, the booming of the great guns continued behind us.

"Go on then, lads!" urged a deep voice from behind us. I turned and found myself face to face with a filthy Uncle Jeb. He stared hard at my face, and we both froze at the ship's railing.

"Good Lord," he whispered. "Abigail?"

I swallowed a lump in my throat and nodded. There was nothing to say, no words to explain the madness of what I had done. The ship lurched again as another British cannonball blasted into the stern.

"Stay with me!" Uncle Jeb shouted, and he held my arm as I climbed over the railing and splashed into knee-deep lake water. The mud sucked at my shoes, and I fell twice trying to run to the shore. The men ahead of us climbed up a bank; some of them had already disappeared into the woods.

I scrambled up the bank as best I could and fell into

line behind the others. Uncle Jeb caught up to me and put a hand on my shoulder.

"Dear God, child," he panted, trying to catch his breath. "What were you thinking...?"

A tree branch snapped back and lashed across my right eye.

"I came to find you," I cried. "I needed to be with family. Papa and Nathan..." I couldn't go on. I could barely keep up with the long-legged man in front of me, and the sobs that threatened to well up from my heart would steal away what little breath I had left.

"I'm sorry," I said quietly.

"You're fortunate," he answered simply. "Aunt Lucy and the boys are back at Crown Point. She's been doing some baking and some healing at times. She'll be heading back to the farm when I return."

I stopped to search his face, but he simply put a hand on my back and pushed me on.

"You'll go with her, of course. We'll talk when we arrive."

Chapter 26

October 13, 1776

Pascal

I hadn't said many prayers in those dark days, but when Abigail turned and faced her uncle, I said a quick one that he would be the kind of man she believed he was. And he was. He hustled us both off that ship and up the bank. I followed them and heard him tell her she could stay with his family. Somehow, I knew this burly, curly-haired, red-faced sailor would welcome a lady who wasn't afraid to get her hands dirty.

Before we headed deeper into the woods, I took a last look back at the *Congress*. She stood in that shallow water, flames licking around her rails, as proud as ever. There was a great blast of an explosion—the powder, I guessed—yet even through the smoke, I could see the colors flying.

I heard a great thump and a loud curse right behind me then. Captain Warner had caught his boot on the tangled roots of a tree. I helped him up, and we marched on.

"We're a lucky crew of rabble," he growled, shaking

his head in amazement.

"We're going to make it then, you think?" I asked. It seemed so strange to be walking alongside him, suddenly. I hadn't seen him except in passing since the day I'd switched boats to serve on the *Spitfire*.

"Through this day, at the least," he answered, and held up a branch so I could duck under it. "The men say you've become quite the sailor," he went on. "Perhaps you'd stay with me if I take on another vessel."

"I don't know," I answered him honestly, but I thought about it as I crunched through the leaves. If James had been right, if we were indeed building something, then I wanted to be part of that.

We came to a place in the woods where the paths broke off in two directions. Ahead of us, I saw Abigail and her uncle take the path to the right. I started to go that way, too, but Captain Warner tugged at my sleeve.

"My crew's been ordered this way," he explained, motioning to the left. "We split up. In case the British catch up with us, at least one group makes it back to Crown Point." He paused. "Would you stay with me?"

There was something in his eyes, or in his tone, or somewhere, that was different this day. Some sort of respect, or affection, or recognition of family. I motioned for him to wait while I ran ahead to catch Abigail.

"We're taking the other trail," I told her, out of breath. She bit her lip and frowned.

"I'm going with Captain Warner," I told her. "I think…I've decided I want to finish. I need to go." It came out all wrong, but she nodded, and I knew she understood. Before the confused eyes of a dozen exhausted sailors, she hugged me.

"You'll build great things, Pascal De Angelis," she whispered in my ear. I could feel warm tears on her cheek against mine before she let go and turned quickly to catch up to her uncle.

I joined Captain Warner on the other trail, and we walked off into the woods.

Abigail

We took our separate paths, the ones we'd been ordered to take. We were soldiers, both of us, and we followed orders. I'd been sent off with Uncle Jeb on the east fork, and Pascal was sent with Captain Warner, still barking at his heels, on the west. I remember pausing, just for a second, for we could hear the British guns growing louder. The trees were already losing their leaves, and I caught a glimpse of him through the branches of a maple, before our two paths wound away from one another. He nodded at me, and I winked, just once, before I turned to follow my uncle to the east.

Epilogue
October 12, 1800

Pascal

All the way south, we had marched peering over our shoulders, expecting to see the Redcoats with their rifles aimed at our hearts. They never did follow, though. Perhaps seeing the strength of the forts gave them second thoughts, especially with winter threatening to come early, as it seems to threaten every year in these parts.

I looked for her at Crown Point. But the place was teeming with men, and I wasn't there for long. Captain Warner shuffled me off onto another vessel with him. He heard we could make more money privateering.

And so we did. There was gold—plentiful gold—but it didn't fill me the way I'd always expected it would. It filled my pockets, surely, but not that place inside that Abigail had opened up.

Today, on my birthday more than two decades later, I remember her.

On all the other ships, all the other trips, I carried her sewing needle, and I etched my stories into life. The powder horn grew crowded with images, each episode in my life huddled up against the next.

It's true, there were grand adventures, and those were the real gold. The gold that stays. I decided to try and turn some of the other kind, the coins, into something real as well.

I purchased some land. Not just me, of course, a few other men, too. But it was a fairly large parcel, enough for a mill or two, a tavern, stores, and houses where families sit down to supper together after the day's work is through.

I decided to do it—to build something.

Epilogue

October 12, 1800

Abigail

I always thought of him on his birthday, though I never knew, really, what happened to him. Of course, I knew that he made it, that he was okay. I can't tell you how I knew. I just did, the way you know some things deep down without learning them, the way the geese know to fly south when the nights get to be cool. He made it. He was all right. Better than all right. I just knew.

I still wanted to know more. I tried writing a couple times but never knew exactly where to send the letter. I knew he stayed with the army a while and had even heard a rumor that he'd been taken captive and thrown in jail in London for a time, to be released when the war ended. I just never knew quite where to write.

I wrote anyway and sent notes off with each messenger who came through town. I never heard back from him. Uncle Jeb and Aunt Mary called him my invisible beau for a time, always laughing as they teased.

They stopped calling him that, and indeed, I stopped writing to Pascal the summer I met Joshua. Truth be told, he had some of the same qualities, the same understated kindness, the same playful sense of humor. And he had some of Nathan's qualities too—his gentleness and protectiveness. We married two springs after we met.

The little ones keep us busy now. James is seven, Christopher four, and Zachary just two and a half.

"A house full of men and our Abby. Good thing

you're such a spitfire, or you'd never survive among this crew!" Aunt Mary always laughs when she visits and sits in the big rocking chair to read to the boys. It's where I always meant to be, in a house like this, playing checkers and hunting for frogs in the pond out back. Truly, by heading out to battle on a wild and frigid lake, I found my way home.

Epilogue

October 12, 1833

Pascal

The village is thriving. Holland Patent, it's called, after the name of our original grant of land. I love to walk the roads and wave at the people who have moved here to work in the mills and open their shops. There are great old oak trees and maples, too. We left them when we cleared the land to build, and they tower over the roads like watchful giants.

I never wrote to Abby. I don't know why, exactly. After the war ended, the whirlwind of a dream coming true swept me up in it.

And of course, there was Ruth. Her family was one of the first to move here when the mill opened. She's an amazing woman, and oh, do we laugh together. Even now, in our golden years, when we can no longer keep up when our grandchildren giggle and want to race, we laugh.

I'm seventy years old today, out for the solitary walk I take every year on October 12. I remember the years that have gone by, and one in particular, always. The year I turned thirteen.

As I turn the corner for home, a flock of geese flies overhead. They honk at me, more than they really need to, I think. I honk back, laugh at myself, and go inside.

Ruth is in the kitchen, and I hear our grandchildren whispering to her about cake. I head straight for the old mahogany desk and pick up a pen.

I have a letter to write.

Epilogue

October 30, 1833

Abigail

The envelope was sealed with the image of an expertly carved gunboat. I knew before I opened it, it was from him. It took fifty-seven years for his letter, but I knew.

I broke the seal and opened it. A single page of parchment was folded inside.

Dear Abigail,

I find myself traveling back in time, this October 12. Do you realize it's been fifty-seven years?

I hope this finds you well. There is so much to say that I don't know where to begin, and yet sometimes words simply aren't enough, no matter where we start or how much ink we spill.

I could tell you that I've had a good life. That after I left you, I fought for our new nation. That I bought land and built a town with mills and stores and best of all, families. That I have a family of my own now— people who make me laugh the way you taught me to laugh so many years ago.

But what I really want to do is thank you. When you rowed up to the side of that gunboat in the wild October waves, I received a precious gift. From you, I learned to care again, to live. I'd been with a fleet of soldiers and sailors for weeks, but it took a twelve-year-old girl to teach me what it meant to be a man.

Epilogue

The image of the Spitfire *on my powder horn will always make me think of you.*

Regards ~
Pascal

Carefully, I put the letter back into its envelope. I lifted the lid of my keepsake trunk and gently laid it inside. It leaned against Papa's powder horn, like an old friend.

I closed the lid and stepped outside. A flock of geese flew overhead, honking and honking. I tilted my head to the warm October sun and laughed.

Author's Note

Historical fiction is one of my very favorite things to read because I love to learn about the past, and I love to get lost in a good story. Like other works of historical fiction, some of the characters in this novel are real historical figures, and some are figures of my imagination. The major events of this book really happened, but because historical documents are limited, I've filled in some of the details, like what was for dinner or what exactly was said at a certain time.

As a reader of historical fiction, I always like to know which parts of the story were real and which parts were imagined or supposed. Here, I've tried to answer some of the questions you might have about *Spitfire*.

Were Abigail and Pascal real?

Pascal De Angelis was a documented crew member in the Battle of Valcour Island. He really was just twelve years old when he joined the fleet with his stepfather, and he really did turn thirteen on October 12, 1776—

the day after the initial battle, when the American ships were fleeing from the British after their escape. Imagine how quickly he must have grown up that year. Many of the details of Pascal's life in this story are also real. His father really did die at sea, and his mother married the ship's captain, who brought Pascal with him to fight on Lake Champlain that fall.

Pascal De Angelis wrote several diary entries about the battle, though historians aren't sure if he actually wrote them down right after the event or later. His diary excerpts were published in the Summer 1974 edition of *Vermont History*. There is also a pension document written by Pascal De Angelis when he was much older. That's a document that a veteran would provide to the government to request a military pension payment. That document tells the story of what happened to Pascal after the Battle of Valcour Island was over. He did indeed continue to serve on ships with his stepfather, Captain Warner. They made some money privateering— capturing enemy ships with the understanding that they could keep any valuables or gold they found.

Eventually, Pascal De Angelis did settle down and build things, as he always dreamed of doing in the story. He founded the village of Holland Patent in Oneida County, which is still there today, a quiet, pretty community with old houses and tall trees. He raised a family and lived there until his death on September 8, 1839. He was seventy-five years old.

Pascal De Angelis is buried in the cemetery in Holland Patent, next to a low stone wall covered with grapevine. His grave is simple but respected and well cared for—a fitting tribute for a man who spent much of his life fighting for his country and started that fight at such a young age.

Abigail Smith is a fictional character. There are no records of any women on the fleet that fought at Valcour Island. There were, however, some women in history who did just what Abigail did—disguised themselves in men's clothing so they could fight in the Revolution.

Deborah Sampson is probably the most famous of these women. She dressed as a man and enlisted in the Continental Army under the name Robert Shurtleff. She fought in several battles and was even wounded without being discovered. Finally, when she was seriously ill with a fever, she had to be treated by a doctor who discovered that she was a woman. He kept her secret at the time, but eventually gave her a note to give to General Washington, which led to her honorable discharge from the army. Deborah Sampson was twenty years old when she enlisted in the army—older than Abigail, but I like to think that if Abby had been real, and if the two young ladies had met, they would have been friends.

Deborah Sampson struggled to keep her true identity hidden, like Abigail. In truth, it probably would have been much more difficult for Abigail, confined as she was to a small boat with more than forty men on board. It's likely that any young woman who did try to sneak on board disguised as a boy would have been discovered sooner than Abigail was. I like to think that Abby was lucky during those days and that the crew was too preoccupied to pay her much attention.

Which other characters were real people in history?

Captain Ulmer was the real-life captain of the *Spitfire*—one of the eight gunboats that took part in the battle. General Waterbury, who commanded the *Washington* until it was surrounded by British ships and forced to surrender, was real, too. He was captured after striking the colors on his ship. Lieutenant Goldsmith, who was injured at the end of the battle, was also a real historical figure. Historians aren't sure what happened to him when the boats ran aground. The crew did what they could to get everyone off the boats, but at least one account reports Goldsmith being left behind when the *Congress* exploded in a flash of powder, her colors still flying.

There really was a poor fellow named Ananius Tubbs, and he really was punished with the cat-o'-nine-tails for sleeping on his watch. How do I know? Another real historical figure named Bayze Wells (who wasn't mentioned in the story) kept a journal during his time with the American fleet on Lake Champlain. On September 22, 1776, his entry reads:

"This day the wind Southerly but small and variable this morning at eight A.M. Ananius Tubbs was cabbed twelve strokes on his naked buttocks for sleeping on his watch. The wind increased at Southwest until night. Lieutenant Fox and Sergeant Whitney made us a visit."

Wells seemed intrigued by the punishments that were handed out around him. Just two days before Mr. Tubbs was disciplined, Wells mentions a man named Ansel

Fox who suffered the same twelve strokes on the behind. He, too, had been sleeping on his watch.

Of course, Benedict Arnold was also a real historical figure, though in this story, he plays a different role than the one for which he is most remembered. Arnold is probably the most famous traitor in American history, and it's true that he committed treason by making plans to hand West Point over to the British in 1780.

What many people don't realize is that before that happened, Arnold was a leader and a hero of the Continental Army. Arnold worked with Ethan Allen to seize Fort Ticonderoga from the British early in the Revolution. He led the raid on Quebec in 1775 (the one from which Abigail's father and brother never returned). And, as you just read, he commanded the American fleet at the Battle of Valcour Island in October of 1776. Benedict Arnold was regarded as even more of a hero the following year, when he led American troops to victory at the Battle of Saratoga—a battle that many historians consider to be a turning point in the war. At Saratoga National Battlefield today, there is a tribute to Arnold—but his name and face are nowhere to be found on the monument. Instead, visitors see a statue of Benedict Arnold's boot—commemorating the leg wound that Arnold received during his heroics at Saratoga, but refusing to honor the man who later became a traitor to his nation.

Who won the Battle of Valcour Island?
Plattsburgh Social Studies teacher Mal Cutaiar tells

his students that the Battle of Valcour Island was "a successful failure." By no means did Benedict Arnold and his crew defeat the British. But they didn't entirely lose the battle either. The goal of building a fleet of boats and putting them on Lake Champlain that summer and fall was to prevent the British from advancing up the lake and taking over American forts at Crown Point and Ticonderoga. Ultimately, that goal was met.

When Arnold ran his remaining boats aground in what is now named Arnold's Bay on the Vermont shoreline, the British fleet turned around and went back to Canada. Perhaps it was because they got a look at just how strong the forts were. Perhaps it was because they could already see the snow on what we now call Mount Mansfield, Vermont's highest peak, and felt the chill of an early winter in the air. For whatever reason, they turned around and didn't come back until the following year. When the standoff finally happened at Saratoga in October of 1777, the American troops were better prepared and ultimately beat the British. The Battle of Valcour Island was a success for the American troops because it bought them the time that they needed.

What happened to the boats that sank during the battle?

Many of them, like the *Congress* and *Royal Savage*, were salvaged from the lake years ago, before we knew much about conservation and historic preservation. These ships were made of wood, and when old wood is pulled from the water and sits out in the elements, it deteriorates and rots quickly. Sadly, these vessels were destroyed.

The *Philadelphia* was raised from the waters of Lake Champlain in 1935, when a diver named Lorenzo Hagglund found the boat and had it brought to the surface. In 1961, it was taken to the Smithsonian Institution in Washington, DC, where it was preserved. If you go there, you can see the *Philadelphia* on exhibit, along with the 24-pound cannonball that caused her to sink.

You can also see what the *Philadelphia* was like by spending a little time on a replica, or exact copy, of the ship that was built by the Lake Champlain Maritime Museum in Vermont and launched in 1991. Today, the *Philadelphia II* is docked at the Maritime Museum in Vergennes, Vermont. You can visit with your family or school group and actually go on board the boat to imagine what it must have been like to live on board in the midst of a battle.

What about the Spitfire*?*

For years, it was assumed to be lost. But in 1997, during the Lake Champlain Maritime Museum's Lake Survey, researchers discovered an intact gunboat resting on the bottom of the lake. Research led them to identify the boat as the *Spitfire*—the last remaining gunboat from Benedict Arnold's fleet. Because the boat was discovered in very deep water, she is incredibly well preserved and incredibly safe, for now. Experts believe the *Spitfire's* resting place is too deep for her to be bothered by divers or zebra mussels, which damage shipwrecks in shallower waters. The gunboat has been identified by the National Trust for Historic Preservation as an American Treasure—a program established to protect and preserve cultural and historical resources like this boat that played such a role in the making of our nation.

What can I see at Valcour Island today?

Today, Valcour Island is owned by New York State and is a beautiful place to hike, fish, kayak, and camp. It's located in Northern New York, just south of Plattsburgh, on Lake Champlain. Many artifacts from the battle have been discovered on the lake bottom between the island and the New York shoreline. Standing on the shore, it's easy to imagine how the American crew members must have felt that night, when they believed that the British fleet had them trapped. You can still hear the waves and imagine musket fire coming from the trees on shore. And if you listen carefully, it's not too difficult to hear echoes of ghosts, especially around a campfire on a cool autumn night.

About the Author

Kate Messner is an author, English teacher, wife, and mother. She attended the S.I. Newhouse School of Public Communication at Syracuse University and worked as a television reporter, covering Northern New York and Vermont before moving on to earn her master's degree in teaching. In 2006, she earned certification from the National Board for Professional Teaching Standards in the area of Early Adolescent English Language Arts.

Kate lives on Lake Champlain with her husband and two children. Depending on the season, she loves to kayak or cross country ski over the waters where the story of the *Spitfire* takes place.

Visit Kate Messner at her website:
www.katemessner.com

Bibliography

The following sources were invaluable to me as I researched *Spitfire* and will be of interest to readers who wish to know more about the Battle of Valcour Island and the American Revolution.

Bellico, Russell P. *Sails and Steam in the Mountains: A Maritime and Military History of Lake George and Lake Champlain.* Fleischmanns, NY: Purple Mountain Press, 1992.

Bird, Harrison. *Navies in the Mountains.* New York: Oxford University Press, 1962.

Clark, William Bell, et al., eds. *Naval Documents of the American Revolution* (8 vols.) Washington, DC, 1964.

Cohn, Arthur. "An Incident Not Known to History: Squire Ferris and Benedict Arnold at Ferris Bay, October 13, 1776." *Vermont History*, 55(2): 97–112, 1987.

Bibliography

De Angelis, Pascale. Pension Document. Historic Preservation
Center at the Holland Patent Free Library.

De Angelis, Pascal "With Benedict Arnold at Valcour Island: The
Diary of Pascal De Angelis." Edited by Charles M. Snyder.
Vermont History, New Ser., 42: 195-200, Summer 1974.

Lundeberg, Philip K. *The Gunboat Philadelphia and the Defense
of Lake Champlain in 1776*. Basin Harbor, VT: Lake
Champlain Maritime Museum, 1995.

Well, Bayze. *Collections of the Connecticut Historical Society*.
Journal of Bayze Wells of Farmington, May, 1775–February,
1777. Hartford: Connecticut Historical Society, 1879.